LOST IN TIME

CHAPTER 1: BACKSTORY

Mike has the ball. He dribbles forward. He steps back. He shoots a three pointer. It goes in. The crowd erupts in cheers. Mike finished the game with all smiles. He had just won the 2022-2023 MVP trophy and was now carrying his team throughout the playoffs. They are destroying the competition.

You may be wondering what happened since Mike hit the game winning shot in the first book of the series, "Ball is Life Jr." Well, life has been going good for Mike. It's been going great for Mike. After hitting the game winning shot, he was a celebrity. He was wealthy and famous. He got a 10-year contract extension, and it looked like he was going to be in the NBA for a while. He still had to go to school, though. Mike was adopted by his agent, and his agent accessed some of Mike's money (with his permission) and bought a nice mansion near San Francisco Bay overlooking the beautiful beach. After rough travels and adventures Mike had experienced his first NBA year, he could finally, hopefully, look forward to a smooth year. After all, he was the NBA MVP. He was playing so well for his team, and everything was coming together. He was so famous just from one shot. He made his own shoes, and even started working on his own clothing brand. He has many endorsements and interviews around the world. He thanked God for all the blessings he had in his life. His life was really coming together.

But that wasn't the case for everyone.

CHAPTER 2: LOST IN LEBANON

15 Years Ago

The couple walked briskly. Rain was pounding on the ground as the couple walked through the dimly lit streets of Lebanon in the night. (If you're wondering, Lebanon is in the Middle East). They were walking fast, without much of a goal. They were carrying a box, with something, or someone, special inside.

The baby whined. "Hush, baby, be quiet. It'll all be alright." said the mother. The father followed behind. After a few minutes of walking, the couple found a tent outside on a grassy area. It seemed as if someone was living there.

"I don't wanna do this. Our baby deserves better." said the mother. "Listen, I know it's tough, but it's our only possibility. It doesn't seem like there is anyone else around that can take care of the baby. The city seems somewhat empty." replied the father. The faint sound of cars honking filled the night sky. The air smelled pretty clean.

The mother looked at her baby. The baby cooed. The baby laughed and smiled. The mother laughed and smiled back. "I'm sorry. I don't want to do this, Daniel." said the mom to the baby. Thunder filled the sky. The mom put the box down with the baby next to the tent. The couple looked at the baby one last time. They turned around and walked away.

The sun quickly rose. It appeared as if there was an old man in the tent. He woke up and got out of his tent. He was startled to see the baby in the box, laughing and smiling. The man, named Vespucci, was surprised. He looked around and didn't see much, just a lot of buildings crowded together. He decided to take the baby and raise him like his own. The first few years passed alright. Vespucci had enough food and water to keep them both stable. There was enough room in the tent for Vespucci and the baby to sleep comfortably. The baby grew pretty fast. At around 2 years old, the baby started saying words. "Daniel. Daniel." said the baby. He remembered his parents calling him that the night he was abandoned. "All right. I will call you Daniel." said Vespucci, smiling. Days, weeks, months, years, passed like this. So similarly. Vespucci realized he was struggling to support himself alone, not even including the now 15-year-old. At this age, Vespucci agreed he was old enough to be left alone. He would leave Daniel at the tent and Vespucci would go around and find work to make some easy money to support him and Daniel. During this, Daniel would wander around and explore the area. He loved walking over to the paper recycling bins. They had so many amazing news articles and pictures he could learn from. That's basically how he learned most things in life. As he was rummaging through paper in the bin, an article caught his attention. It was by Sports Illustrated. Daniel picked it up. He saw a picture of a basketball player shooting a basketball shot. The player seemed really young compared to the rest of the players. Daniel looked at the caption. It said, "Mike Johnson succeeds on the three pointer over LeBron James to win the 2021-2022 NBA championship!!". Daniel was interested. It seems like this Mike Johnson guy is a good player, Daniel thought. He grabbed the article and walked over to his tent. He sat down and began reading the article. He really enjoyed the section where he read about Mike Johnson, the boy on the cover.

"Meet Mike Johnson. He has an incredible journey from regular kid to NBA MVP and Champion. His journey started out with the opportunity of a lifetime. He competed against thousands of kids for a chance to meet and train with NBA legends. And Mike made it. Out of those 5 kids selected, only 1 kid would be selected to play in an official NBA game of his choice. And Mike made that. He got an incredible chance to play an NBA game with the Golden State Warriors, dropping 10 points and the game winning shot for the W. Of course, it was supposed to stop there. But it didn't. The fans loved him so much that Mike got the chance to sign an NBA contract, becoming the youngest player in the history of the NBA – and probably all of professional sports. After this, things turned down for Mike. As Mike claims, he was kidnapped and sent to Iraq. He survived by driving away from practically the whole Iraqi military and jumping out of a car and parachuting to safety. He got to the Baghdad, Iraq airport and tried to travel back to America. However, the plane door broke open and Mike slid out. Thank God he had a parachute to grab on to. He put it on and used it to glide into wild Africa. He survived countless days in the prairies of Africa, running away from wild animals and jumping off mountains and gliding to safety. He finally found civilization but had to escape in a van. He hoped the van would take him to the nearest airport. Mike fell out though, in the middle of the Sahara Desert. He walked for many days until he finally arrived at the airport. He got onto a plane and arrived in New York, New York City, and took a ride to Los Angeles, California. He got everything sorted out and carried his team from down 3-0 in all series to the NBA championship games. They were also down 3-0, but Michael Johnson dropped countless points to bring his team back up to 3-3 against the Cleveland Cavaliers. In Game 7, the Warriors found themselves down 30 in the 4th quarter. Mike brought his team back up with multiple shots. He then hit the greatest shot in NBA history to win the game. Mike won the 2022 NBA Finals MVP, and the Golden State Warriors won the 2022 NBA championship. Mike became so famous and even has his own brand right now. To this day, Mike won the 2023 NBA regular season MVP, averaging 35 points, 11 assists, and 11 rebounds per game. Right now, he is helping his team find a spot in the NBA championship series games. When asked for inspiration, Mike attributes all his help to God. He says how much God helped him and that you should find and trust God too in order to live your best life!!".

Daniel enjoyed the article. He liked how Mike had went from struggles to success. He gave Daniel hope, as he was living through struggles right now. Daniel decided that if Mike could make it out of bad situations, so could Daniel. So can Daniel. Mike decided that when the time was right, he would work super hard to get enough money to travel to the United States of America and look for career and life opportunities. Of course, he had to bring Vespucci with him. Little did Daniel know that he would have to work even harder through the harder times coming soon.

CHAPTER 3: DEPARTURE

Daniel was eagerly waiting for Vespucci to arrive at the tent, with food and water. As the sun was nearing to set, Dan walked around and walked towards the nearby apartments. He noticed the glare of the television reflecting through someone's window. Dan walked up intrigued. And that's when he saw it for the first time.

Basketball.

He loved it. He watched how the players ran up and down the courts, dribbling and passing the ball in fancy ways, scoring through mid-range shots, 3-pointers, layups, and awesome dunks. He then realized he was watching Michael Johnson play as well. He is an amazing player, thought Daniel. He didn't realize how much time passed. After a few hours it was past midnight. "Daniel! Daniel!" yelled Vespucci. Daniel looked around. He ran back to Vespucci. "Sorry, I was just watching basketball.". said Daniel. Vespucci smiled. "It's ok" he said. Daniel sat down and looked at the sky. "So, what did you get today?" he asked. "Not much. Just a few dollars but something special.". Vespucci pulled something out of his pocket. It was a vintage-looking watch. "I want you to have this.". Daniel took the watch. He put it on. He thought it was an alright gift. "Goodnight, Daniel. I'll miss you." said Vespucci, with a serious tone. As Daniel layed down to sleep, he wondered why he said he'd miss him. Maybe Vespucci will miss Daniel as he is at work the next day. As Daniel was sleeping, he heard noises. He heard lots of vehicles driving up and heard lots of talking. He heard the vehicles leave. Daniel assumed it was a dream.

Daniel wakes up. He looks around and realizes Vespucci left early. Way earlier than usual. He guessed that Vespucci was probably going to work earlier to make more money. And that's when Daniel saw the note.

"Daniel, it's Vespucci. I'm sorry it has to be this way. I was drafted by the Lebanese military. We are going to fight a war in Russia. I had to do this because I was forcefully drafted. At least I'll make some money. I probably won't ever see you again. I love you, Daniel. Even though you aren't my biological son, I love you more than ever. You are great to me. You give me hope. I know that one day you will make me proud by finding a good job somewhere, like America, making millions of dollars. I just hope you don't forget about me. By the time you are reading this, I'm probably already in the plane to Russia. Now go, find another family to live with if they will accept you. Also, look for a job. Try to save enough money to get a plane ticket to America. Anyways, I wish you the best of luck. Trust God.

-Best, Vespucci

Daniel froze. He didn't know what to do. He didn't know what to say. He was at a loss for words. He flipped the note over. It was written on the page with Mike Johnson and the story of his success. He read about how his family betrayed him and how he had to survive in the wild. This was kind of the situation Daniel was in. He decided he had to pack up and leave. He didn't have much money, just the watch Vespucci gave him. He left the tent where it was, packed up some food and water bottles, and set out on a journey.

He had a plan. A crazy plan, but a plan that would be revolutionary. He decided to sneak onto a plane to America and somehow try to meet Mike. He would tell Mike his story and ask for help. Maybe Mike would help him. He had to.

Daniel walked for a few hours until he finally reached the downtown of Beirut, Lebanon. He was exhausted and found a bench to rest on. He had some food and water and went to sleep.

The next morning, Daniel got a taxi. He asked to go to the airport. He arrived after a few hours of traffic. He pays the driver with some money he found on the ground. He got his stuff and left the taxi.

Daniel looks around. He grabs his bag with food and water and walks into the airport. He goes to the big screen to see upcoming flights. He notices one going to Pennsylvania, U.S.A. from Beirut, Lebanon. He sees that it is Flight 248. He grabs his watch to check the time. It says 2:48 P.M. on it. He looks at the airport screen. It says 11:18 A.M. He realized the watch was probably broken and likely worthless. He decided to keep it though. It was his only memory of Vespucci, along with the letter that Daniel has. He decides to walk over to the gate for Flight 248. Luckily, he blends in with the crowd easily. As a family is checking into the airport, Daniel tries to stick with him as if they were his family. He wished he had his family. He still didn't understand why his parents left him in a box near Vespucci's tent. At least Vespucci raised him right.

Daniel walked onto the plane. "Hi, who are you with?" asked a flight attendant at the entrance. "Hi, I'm with them." said Daniel as he followed the family. He walked onto the plane. The family looked at him momentarily, confused. Daniel walked around the plane and found an open seat. He sat down. He was surprised how easy it is for kids to get onto a plane. According to Mike, he had done this multiple times. After a few minutes, the plane had taken off. Dan was hungry and thirsty, so he ordered some food and water. After eating he decided to nap for a little. He woke up and felt the plane shaking. People in the plane were getting up and panicking. Daniel had no idea what was going on. He looked outside the window and saw the engine exploding and on fire. We're going to crash, he thought. I should've stayed in Lebanon, he thought. He looked outside and saw a huge area of snowy mountains approaching. The plane was directed towards the mountains. He got up and tripped. The watch slipped out of his pocket. He ran after it as one side of the plane broke off. The watch was blown out of the plane and was flying into the mountains. The plane got even closer to the mountains. He had seconds left before a possible collision. Dan closed his eyes.

CHAPTER 4: LOST

Daniel woke up. He felt kind of dizzy. It didn't take him long to realize he was in the middle of a forest. Danny got up and looked around for where the plane could've crashed. He searched for a few minutes and realized the plane was nowhere near him. He wondered how he even survived the plane crash. He wondered if the plane even crashed. He didn't feel it crash. If it crashed and he survived, he would have felt the impact. He remembered closing his eyes in the plane and opening them a few seconds later, with nothing happening. It was as if he teleported out of the plane to safety. He pondered for a few minutes and decided to get up and look around. He walked for miles and couldn't see any civilization. As he was walking, he was startled as an arrow flew by him and hit a tree near him. Daniel jumped. He looked behind him and saw a man on a horse, pointing a bow and arrow at him. "Hello? I'm not here to do anything, I'm just lost. I think my flight crashed. Can you help me?" asked Daniel. The man brought his horse closer to Daniel. As he approached, he realized something. The man was dressed as a Native American.

Daniel remembering reading an article about Native tribes that still exist to this day. Danny just guessed the plane landed fine and they left Danny in the middle of the forest, near a tribal location. The native still didn't respond but left with his horse. Daniel decided to follow. After a few minutes of walking, Dan saw the civilization. He saw lots of huts and lots of Native Americans. He assumed this was where the native tribes were. He hoped he could get help to find the nearest airport so he could clear up what happened to Flight 248 and find his way to California. As Dan walked into the land, the Natives stared at him weirdly. Dan didn't say anything. He noticed a shore nearby, and he walked to the shore. He sat down and stared out at the ocean. It was probably the Atlantic Ocean, if he actually landed in Pennsylvania. He couldn't understand how he survived the crash, if there even was a crash. He checked his pockets, and still had the letter from Vespucci. He didn't have the watch though. He last saw it flying towards the mountains. After a few minutes, Dan saw something. He saw a figure in the ocean, sailing closer and closer. He realized it was a ship. He then saw 2 other ships behind it.

As the ships got closer, he realized that there were Britian's flags on the ships. He realized the main ship in front had the word "Mayflower" on the ship. It seemed like a familiar name, something he had read from an article from a recycling bin. When the ships got closer, Daniel saw there were people on the ship. They had powdered wigs and were dressed like colonists for some reason. And there was one man standing in front and seemed to be the leader. He looked familiar. And that's when Daniel realized. It was Christopher Columbus. This was when Britain accidentally discovered America on a trip to find more routes to India.

Daniel looked around and didn't see any cameras. This couldn't be a movie. And that's when Daniel realized.

He was in the year 1492.

CHAPTER 5: LOST IN TIME

Daniel was scared. He was about to experience a historical moment firsthand, hundreds of years ago. He got out the article still in his pocket. The front page had the letter from Vespucci, and the article about Michael Johnson. Daniel flipped the page over. It had an article about a watch.

"This watch is not what it seems. Sure, it seems old, but it has magical powers. The watch doesn't even tell the time, but it is fabled to have time-traveling powers. It was apparently created by the Egyptians thousands of years ago but was lost for thousands of years. Finally, the watch was reported to be found in present-day Beirut, Lebanon. It is not known who now has the watch. While it has time-traveling powers, not many know how to activate it. It is interesting to think how life changing this watch could be for humanity if its powers are used."

Daniel looked at the picture of the watch. It was the same as the watch Vespucci gave him. Daniel was shocked. And then he realized. When the watch slipped out of his pocket, it fell somewhere in the mountains. Dan closed his eyes and woke up. So, it possibly time-traveled him back to 1492, which made sense as colonists were arriving in America. So, Daniel now knew his new task. He had to go to the mountains and find his watch. He looked over at the mountains and saw they were far. He decided he had to go find his watch, find out how to go back to the future and find his way to Mike. He should've just stayed in Lebanon. Daniel just didn't know what to do. He was standing for a solid 10 minutes, just thinking. And then the ships arrived.

"Hello! We are here on an expedition. It appears we have discovered a new land. Who are you people?" asked Christopher Columbus. Daniel was scared. "Uh, don't ask me. Can you help me get to the mountains". Christopher stared. "I'm just confused. We come in peace.". Daniel ran. He ran back through the forests. He saw the colonists chasing him. He didn't know why he ran, but he didn't know what to do. He hoped he could find some Native Americans that could get him some food and water for his journey, and maybe a horse, to get to the mountains. Daniel was running and ran into someone. He fell. He looked up and saw a Native American. Soon, he was surrounded by Natives. "Please, I just want food, water, and transportation to the mountains. I'll leave you alone.". They didn't understand them. Daniel pointed at his stomach, pointed at his mouth, and stuck out his tongue to show he was hungry and thirsty. He pointed at the horse, then pointed at the mountains. The Natives nodded in agreement. The colonists ran in. "Hey? Who are you people?" asked Colombus. The Natives froze. They stared back at Daniel. He backed away. It was quiet for a few seconds. Then a battle broke out. Daniel took advantage of the chaos. He went to a pond and drank as much water as he could. He grabbed a bag and put vegetables in it.

He hopped on a horse and used the reigns to guide it towards the mountains. "AY"! The Natives yelled. They went on their horses and started chasing Daniel down. Arrows whizzed past him.

Daniel was having a hard time navigating with the horse. The horse seemed well trained, so it followed in a straight path towards the mountains. Danny was having a hard time holding on to the horse. The Natives kept shooting arrows near Mike but thank God they missed. Daniel saved some time by taking a detour through some trees to escape the Native Americans. The horse kept galloping and then suddenly stopped. Daniel looked down. He saw a ravine that looked really deep, with flowing rivers and water going through fast. Dan heard multiple horses coming close. Dan saw the mountains were on the other side of the mountains. Dan got off. The same Native American chief that he first saw in the forest arrived and got off his forest. He pointed a bow and arrow at Daniel seriously. Daniel looked back at the ravine. He jumped. It felt like a rollercoaster as he was in the air for a few seconds before colliding with the cold water. Daniel got up quickly and ran to the shore of the river. He looked up and saw rocks he could grab onto to climb up to the base of the mountain. He looked back at the Natives and saw them leaving. Daniel struggled to climb up, but barely did it. He was exhausted. He realized he left the food with the horse. He sighed. He decided his only choice was to find the watch and time travel to 2022 and find some food, and then go to the airport and get to Mike Johnson. Daniel spent several hours walking around the base of the mountain and searching for the watch. He was getting cold, and dusk was approaching. Just as Daniel was losing hope, a gleam of light reflected into Daniels eyes. He squinted and realized the sun was at the right angle to reflect off of something. He looked forward and saw a small, gold-looking object that was reflecting the sun's light. That had to be the watch. Daniel trudged through the snow, climbed up rocks, and made his way to the light. At last, he realized it was the watch. He screamed in happiness. He picked it up. It looked the same as it had before. Daniel clicked many buttons in many patterns trying to find a way to take him forward in time. He then remembered how he even travelled back in time. The watch collided with a mountain, and it took him back in time. He decided to throw the watch against the mountain. He threw it as well as he could against the mountains. It seemed like nothing happened. And then he heard the stomping of what seemed like a massive creature. He looked behind him and jumped. He saw a dinosaur. A real dinosaur. A stegosaurus literally walking in front of him, stomping the ground with force. And that's when Daniel realized he accidentally time traveled millions of years ago.

CHAPTER 6: JURASSIC AGE

Daniel didn't know what to do. Sure, he could time-travel, but he didn't know how to decide the time. It seemed random. He hoped he could find a way back to the future if that was possible. If not, maybe he could time-travel to Ancient Egypt and find the creator of the watch and ask them how to control it. Daniel didn't want to mess around with the dinosaurs, so he decided to go look for the watch and time travel again. He heard a screech. He looked up and saw a velociraptor heading towards him. Dan yelled, ran, and jumped off the side of a mountain. He tumbled down snow and landed in the snow. He got up, cold and wet. He trudged through the snow and jumped down from rock to rock on the mountains. He felt the cold and strong breezes. Daniel had to find the watch and keep trying until he either arrived in Ancient Egypt or found his way back to the future. Daniel didn't even know how time travel could even be possible. He took a deep breath and kept trudging through the snow. As he was walking, he looked up at the sky. He saw a glaring figure that seemed to be moving closer and closer to Earth. Dan didn't know what that could possibly be. And then he realized. That had to be the asteroid that wiped out the dinosaurs. It was moving closer and closer. Daniel guessed that the watch not only time traveled him, but to famous events in history, like the discovery of America and the dinosaurs being wiped out. Daniel had to find the watch and escape first before the asteroid arrived. Daniel finally got to the bottom of the mountain. He found some fruits and water and decided to eat and drink. He felt fine after the food. He didn't even realize he had fallen asleep. When Daniel woke up, he was sweating. He looked over at the mountain, and saw the snow was melting fast and was turning into water. Daniel looked up and saw the asteroid surprisingly close to the mountain. Daniel was sweating. He had to work quickly to find the watch. He was frightened. Daniel was looking around. He started jogging. He started running. He was panicking as the asteroid was moving closer and closer. It was minutes away. Daniel ran as fast as he could near the mountains. He saw a gleam. Daniel got closer. Thank God it was the watch. Daniel screamed in happiness. He grabbed the watch. He threw it at the mountain. Nothing happened for a few seconds. And then, the asteroid came. Daniel watched as it collided with the ground. A huge rumble put Dan in the air, and waves of fire and heat blew through the area. Daniel collided with the ground and fell asleep.

CHAPTER 7: MEDIEVAL TIMES

Daniel got up. He looked around. He heard the chattering of people. He was dizzy. He layed down and found himself in a pile of hay. He looked up hazily. He was in a pile of hay being towed by horses. He looked around and saw lots of medieval looking houses, and he seemed to be in the downtown area. There were many shops, people going for food, and there was a lot of activity. He heard people speaking in a British accent. He saw men in chain suits on horses, galloping through the city. Children ran around and played. Adults carried lots of silver and gold coins, and payed for food. Adults were handwashing clothes and leaving them outside to dry. It was pretty clear to Daniel that he had now time travelled to Europe in the Medieval era. He didn't know the year. He guessed it was somewhere between the 400s and the 1800s. He got out of the cart, fatigued. People stared at him in confusion. He walked into a store. "Hi, I'm new here. Could I get some food?" asked Daniel. "That'll be 4 coins. Where ya from, mate?" asked the shop owner. "I don't have money." said Daniel. "No food then. Sorry mate." said the shop owner. Daniel sighed. He left the shop. He went to a small pond and drank some water. It tasted musty. He went back up to the town. He decided he could look for the watch and hope for better. He went back to the crate and saw the watch in the hay. He picked it up. He looked at it and saw something in the reflection. A horse bumped into him. He fell to the ground and dropped the watch. A soldier in a chain suit got off the horse and picked up the horse. "Everyone come 'ere!" said the soldier. "I found em! The watch from Egypt. The legend. Oi, I found it!" said the soldier. "Bring it to the King! He will reward you greatly." said a townsperson. "That's right. And look at this thief here.". The soldier looked down at Daniel. "He stole the watch from Egypt, somehow. But it's ok. I'll sell the watch to the King and take this filthy thief into the dungeons! I will be famous!" yelled the soldier. Everyone started cheering. Another soldier picked up Daniel and tied his hands together. He was thrown back into the cart and was tied to the cart. The soldier hopped on the horses and started taking them. They soon left the town and travelled through rural lands. It felt like hours of traveling. Of course, this had to happen to Daniel. He found the watch and had it stolen from him and was now going to be trapped in a dungeon by the King of

England. Daniel didn't know why this was happening to him. Why did time travel even exist?? He felt like he was travelling for hours, and he was getting extremely hungry. As night approached, he got up and looked around. He saw lots of people traveling through a huge path through land, seeming to trade. There was a sign that said "Silk Road". So, this was the famous Silk Road from history. Sure, it's cool that he was experiencing historical events. But he was on the wrong side of history. Finally, he arrived. The horse carriage stopped. Daniel got up and looked around. He was right in front of a huge and majestic castle. Soldiers ran down and grabbed Daniel. They forced him to walk up the ton of stairs to the castle entrance. They threw Daniel onto the area in front of the door onto a carpet. Soldiers began rolling down the door. The huge door opened, and inside stood a man wearing a silky and luxurious robe. He had a crown and was surrounded by soldiers. The soldier holding Daniel bowed. "Nice to see you, King. We found something amazing.". The soldier gave the watch to King James. He inspected it. "This can't be.... the time traveling watch?" asked the King. The soldier nodded. "This thief had it in that old village in West England. We took him and traveled here to give you this watch, which is probably worth millions of dollars.". The King stared at Daniel. "I'll be keeping this. Let's test it out soon. As for this filth? Lock him up now.". They picked up Daniel. They carried him into the castle and down a flight of stairs. They arrived in the dungeon. It was super dusty. He was thrown into a room. The bars were closed on him and locked. The only sunlight he had was a small hole in the rocks.

Daniel was beginning to starve. He was getting thirsty, too. There was nothing at all inside the room, except for himself. He just sat down and stared at the ceiling. Daniel started shaking the bars and yelling. Nothing happened.

This wasn't even fair. Vespucci gave him this watch as a gift. He didn't know it had time travel capabilities and was so looked-out for. If it weren't for the watch, Daniel would probably be in California right now, talking to Mike Johnson.

Somehow, Daniel fell asleep. When he woke up, he saw there was a plate with stale bread on it and a cup of water. He ate it, even though it didn't taste the best. He was still hungry. He kept shaking the bars. He felt them getting slightly looser. He kept kicking the walls. Small pieces of rock broke off, and dust filled the air. He peeped through the little hole and looked outside. He saw grass, and a huge lake in front. He just wanted to leave and get the watch. His goal was to get to Egypt and find a way back to the future. A guard walked up to the cage to see how Daniel was doing. "What year is it?" asked Daniel. The guard stared back. "1500.". Daniel stopped. He was in the year 1500. He didn't know what to do with that information. The guard left. Daniel was probably going to be there for another few hours without food. For the following days, Daniel would eat a meal of bread and water, and then would shake and kick the dungeon doors as much as he could. Every day, it got looser. After 10 days (about 1 and a half weeks) in the dungeon, Daniel was getting exhausted. He hasn't eaten or slept properly in probably 2 weeks. Finally, on Day 10, it happened. Daniel was shaking and kicking the door as much as he could. He was shaking and kicking it more aggressively than he ever had. He kept shaking the door until it finally fell loose and broke off. It collided with the ground and made a loud sound as dust flew through the air. Daniel coughed. He heard yelling from the floor above. He heard the clattering of footsteps as soldiers ran down the stairs. Daniel bolted the other way. He entered another room and found a stairway that led outside. He ran onto the lawn. He saw a ladder leading up to a high window, so he climbed up. He kept his balance and jumped into a small room. There wasn't anyone in it. He looked outside the window and saw soldiers starting to climb up the ladder. Daniel ran out of the room and closed the door. He ran through many hallways until he found the main stairways. He climbed up as high as he could until he got to the top floor. He ran down another hallway near a huge room. He slid and stopped in front of the door. It was slightly open. He ran back to the stairways. He looked down at the other levels and saw soldiers running around frantically. Hopefully they won't find Daniel soon. Daniel crept slowly to the entrance of the huge room. He peeked in and saw the King talking to another man. He looked at the other man and saw him holding a wearable contraption that had wings on the back. Daniel listened to the conversation. "Leonardo, you are a wonderful artist. I appreciate all the paintings you have given me. I would also like you to give me that flying machine. I have something to give you as well." said the King. Daniel realized that it was Leonardo DaVinci. The King picked up a box and opened it. Inside was the watch. Daniel felt a gust of air blow through the window. And then he saw a plane. It would be difficult, but he could run in, take the watch, take the contraption, put it on, and jump out the window and hope it works. Maybe he could glide somewhere safe to time travel. Daniel had to get the King distracted. Dan ran to the stairways. The soldiers were looking for him. "HEY! I'M HERE!!" yelled Daniel. The soldiers looked up and yelled. They started running up the stairs. Daniel ran back and found a room to hide in. The soldiers ran to the King's room. "Sorry to interrupt, your majesty, but the prisoner has escaped!!". The King stopped. "GET THAT PRISONER!!" yelled King furiously. He started running away from the room, looking for Dan. Leonardo followed. Daniel checked if the coast was clear. Once he could go, he ran into the room. He grabbed the watch out of the box. He put it in his pocket. He saw the wearable plane. He picked up a pamphlet near it. It had diagrams of the plane and what seemed to be instructions, but the words were written backwards. Daniel remembered learning that Leonardo wrote backwards to avoid people stealing his work. Danil saw straps, and he put them on over his shoulders and back. It fits comfortably. The plane was on his back, and proper. He stood on the window ledge. Daniel stares out into the landscape. Just then, the King barges into the room. Daniel turns around. They stared at each other. "This is for history. Tell Leonardo I say thanks.". Daniel jumps. He feels the cold wind. He pulls the lever, and the wings open. He is pulled up and glides through the air. The contraption was working! It was easy to maneuver. He was gliding forward at a fast rate. "FIRE!". Daniel heard something whizzing through the air. He looked behind him and saw a huge cannonball heading towards him. Daniel panicked as the cannonball collided with one of the wings on the contraption. It broke off and Daniel was losing control. He was spiraling down very fast. He grabbed the watch and threw it as he was going down. He kept going. He closed his eyes. He collided. He fell through trees and bushes and rolled down hills. He came to a stop after a rough tumble. He got up and saw himself in a familiar forest. He heard someone running, and something galloping following them.

CHAPTER 8: DON'T MESS WITH TIME

Daniel got scared and got up very quickly. He hid behind a tree. He peeked out and saw a boy trip and fall to the ground. A Native American on a horse stopped. Daniel realized who the boy was. It was him. Daniel was staring at Daniel.

And then he realized. Somehow, the time travel watch had brought Daniel back to the past not only in history, but in Daniel's history. Daniel was back in 1492, but he realized that Daniel was now a part of history. If he had time travelled back to the places he had already been, then he would have been there since he was now a part of history. He didn't realize how much of an effect on history he could have. Daniel saw himself get up and talk to the Native. He started walking towards the tribe. Daniel had to go find the watch. If the old Daniel sees the new Daniel, it could affect history in crazy ways. Daniel started walking through the forests near the mountains to see where the watch ended up now. After a few hours of searching, he saw the watch. He was running into it but ran into someone. He looked and saw he ran into himself. Daniel stared at him. He yelled and ran. "Oh no," said Daniel. The other Dan was looking for the watch, and they ran into each other. Daniel just saw himself, which wasn't supposed to happen. The old Daniel saw the new Daniel. The timeline was going to be messed up. Daniel picked up the watch and threw it. He teleported to a field. He looked out and saw himself gliding through the air. A cannon broke off a wing and Daniel started spiraling down. Daniel was seeing himself in the Medieval times event, which had just happened. Daniel, wearing the plane contraption, looked down and saw himself. He yelled. He grabbed the watch and threw it. Daniel watched as Daniel, himself, collapsed through the bushes and teleported. Now the other Daniel that he scared was going to teleport back to the year 1492 as the new Daniel had just had. But now, there will be three Daniels. The first Daniel, his first time traveling (year 1492), the second Daniel, the one that scared the other Daniel by seeing himself, and the third Daniel, the one who saw himself on the ground as he was flying, spiraling. Daniel realized that the pattern would keep going on. Just then, a fourth Daniel appeared. They looked at each other. Daniel was frightened. Daniel looked up at the castle and saw himself jumping off with the contraption. It wasn't supposed to happen again, since it only happens once in each timeline. He time traveled and now events were happening multiple times in a row. Daniel that was flying, looked down and saw the two Daniels staring up at him. He yelled. The cannon collided with both wings this time. Since Daniel was scared, he moved too much and had both wings damaged, instead of the one wing damaged like last time when Daniel wasn't scared. He was falling straight down. "Throw the watch!" yelled Daniel. The other Daniel didn't listen and fell through the bushes. Daniel picked up the watch from his pocket. It disappeared in his hands. The other Daniel that fell through the bushes must have broken the watch as he fell. Since Daniel flying had to originally time travel to 1492 again, and back to medieval times, the watch was what got him there. But now the watch was broken. Daniel had no way to go back in the past or in the future. If that doesn't make sense, let me explain: Let's say a building is created in the year 2 AD. In the year 700 AD, the building is still standing. However, if someone goes back to the year 2 AD and destroys it, the building won't be in the year 700 AD anymore. Since it was destroyed from the timeline, it doesn't exist to be in 700 AD since it was destroyed before that year, in 2 AD. The same type of thing was going on with the watch. Now Daniel had no way to go back in time to stop the watch from being broken, because the watch was the only thing that could go back in time to stop the watch from being broken. At least, that's what Daniel thought. He ran to the bushes to check on the other Daniel. "Are you okay?" asked Daniel 1 (the original main character that went through the experiences first.). "I'm okay" said Daniel 2 (the other Daniel that was scared by the original Daniel, causing him to fly and break the watch). "You got some explaining to do" said Daniel 3 (the other Daniel that appeared and watched Daniel 2 fly, as Daniel 1 watched as well). Daniel 1 stopped. "So, I messed up. I saw myself as I was traveling through time. That messed up the timeline, and now you're here, Daniel 3. Daniel 2, you weren't supposed to see me. You were supposed to land with one wing and teleport. But now, the watch is broken because you got scared by seeing us, we are you, watching you fly." Daniel 2 took the watch out of his pocket. It was crumpled and destroyed. Daniel 2 started talking. "It was my first-time by time traveling. I was on the plane and found myself in the forest. I saw a Native American. I saw Christopher Colombus arrive. A battle started, and I ran to look for the watch. But I ran into you, Daniel 1. I panicked and picked up the watch and clicked a button and threw the watch. It brought me here.". Daniel 1 paused. "Yeah. That wasn't supposed to happen. You were supposed to find your own watch in the mountains, teleport to the Jurassic Era, and teleport to a town in Europe and escape. That's what I went through. But you bumped into me and picked up my watch, and you brought us both here. It's kind of my fault. I should have made sure you wouldn't see me, and I should have made sure you got your own watch to continue the timeline. Well, now what?" said Daniel 1. "I know what." said a man. He walked out of the forest. He also looked like Daniel. Let's call him Daniel 4. "So, you scared 2 Daniel's. The first Daniel was me, Daniel 4. You scared me but I still teleported back to 1492 and back here, just like you, Daniel 1. However, the second Daniel, which is Daniel 2, didn't get to teleport because his watch broke." said Daniel 4. "Okay, I'm sorry I broke the watch. But to be fair, I did get scared." said Daniel 2. "Okay. Here's the plan. We just got to accept we are the same people. I have a plan. We travel together and go to Egypt. We can ask the maker to fix our watches. Then, all four of our watches will be fixed since the original watch will be fixed in the timeline." said Daniel 2. Everyone agreed. And then it began. They started their long travel to Egypt.

CHAPTER 9: JOURNEY TO ANCIENT EGYPT

They started walking over the fields. As night approached, Daniel saw a star that pointed towards the South Pole. If he followed it, then he would go south. He wanted to go south since Egypt is south of Europe. And so, it began. The four Daniels started their journey down to Egypt. They talked a bit and had everything in common for the most part. After all, they were all the same person. They travelled for days, stopping to rest on some grass. Daniel felt like Mike once did. He remembered how Mike had been stranded in Africa and had to travel across the rainforests and prairies. Daniel felt like he was in a similar situation. At least he wasn't alone. He had himself – literally 3 other people. And he had God. After they rested, they kept walking. They were walking in wide open areas of grass. For miles they could see, it was all grass and hills. The weather was nice. The scenery they travelled through looked too good to be true. The sky was a bright blue with a few clouds. The weather felt like a crisp 74 degrees. The grass was moist and bright green. There were a few trees here and there, but the grass was spotless overall. Not many insects or animals, and lots of hills. There were some mountains in the distance. He didn't know Europe was this beautiful. He wondered what the area would look like at the present time. He was walking through the hills in the 1500s. By the 2000s, the land would probably be settled and filled with factories, shops, stores, houses, and more. Daniel just took it all in. After walking more through miles and miles of grass and hills, the Daniels settled to sleep on the grass. Daniel looked up at the spotless sky and saw the beautiful stars and comets. He could faintly see what looked like the Northern Lights, which is more visible from Northern Europe. They slept well and kept going.

After nearly 2 days without food or water, the Daniels were in serious need of nourishment. At last, they found a pond surrounded by trees with apples. They drank as much water and ate as many apples as they could. It wasn't much, but they were satisfied. Thank God they could survive. They kept walking when they saw something that caught their attention. They saw what looked like a village, with a few buildings and a lot of people. They yelled in excitement and sprinted towards the village. Once they got closer, they realized how much bigger it really was. Once they got closer, they saw a map. It showed that they were in the very bottom of Italy. Daniel looked and saw that only water separated them and Egypt. They could somehow find a boat that could take them right to Egypt, though Daniel. "Alright guys, we made it. Let's go find an inn, get some rest, and create a plan to get to Egypt." said Daniel 1. They all agreed. They walked to a store that had a sign on it, in what seemed like Italian. It said "Le Locanda". Daniel 1 walked up to the shop owner. "Hello, sir, what is this?". In a heavy Italian accent, the man responded. "Zis is the, the locanda. You, zuh, stay here." said the man. "So, is this like an inn? Hotel?" asked Daniel 1. "Zes, it is. Would zu like to purchaze a ticket?". Daniel 1 looked at the other Daniels. He looked back at the man. "Yes.". The shop owner grabbed a bag. "That will be, zuh, 50 coins for ze one night stay." said the man. "I don't have any." said Daniel 1. "Wait, hold on." said Daniel 3. He grabbed the broken watch from his pocket. "I know we will get this fixed, but this gold piece isn't necessary. It doesn't help the watch function; it is just for design so maybe we can sell this to stay here and eat." said Daniel 3. "Smart idea" said Daniel 4. Daniel 2 went to the shop owner. "Do you take gold?" he asked. "No, I don't. You must go to ze pawn zhop and ask if you can zell it for ze money." said the owner. The Daniels walked over to the pawn shop. "Hello, sir, would you take this gold piece?" asked Daniel 2. The store owner grabbed the piece and examined it. "Zis looks familiar. From ze famous watch that zupposedly has time-traveling powers. Have you seen zat?" asked the owner, intently. "No" Daniel 2 quickly responded. The shop owner stared, confused. "Okay. I can do 100 coins for zis." said the owner. They traded and got the coins. They went to the hotel owner and bought a one-night stay that supplied nourishment. As Daniels 2,3, and 4 got settled in the hotel room, Daniel 1 went for a walk. He wanted to use the other 50 coins to buy a boat ticket to Italy. As he was walking around, he saw a man putting up posters on stores. Daniel went up and took one off. It had a picture of his face and said "WANTED. REWARD: $1,000,000,000. COURTESY OF KING JAMES OF ENGLAND". No way. The King put a billion-dollar reward on Daniel, just to get a stupid watch back? It was broken anyways. Just then, Daniel heard trumpets fanfare in the background. He saw a huge crowd of people. Tons of soldiers were marching and there was an escort of horses carrying a luxurious-looking carriage. A man looked out of the carriage. It was King James of England. Daniel grabbed as many posters as he could and sprinted back to the hotel. He ran upstairs to the hotel room. "What happened?" asked Daniel 2. He showed him the poster. "Oh no." said Daniel 3.". "Look outside. Who's that?" asked Daniel 4. "That's King James of England. If all went right, you were supposed to time travel to him and escape and fly and teleport. You picked up my watch when we ran into each other in 1492, so you didn't get to teleport correctly in the order we did." said Daniel 1.

"ATTENTION, ALL!" said King James. "I am sure you are all aware of a man called Daniel. As you can see in the posters, I am offering a 1-billion-dollar reward for anyone who can find Daniel. He has the time-traveling watch, and I need it!" said the King. Just then, the pawn shop owner and the hotel owner ran to the King. "Zir, we zaw Daniel. 4 of zem! Zey looked zo zimilar, zo they must have been identical twins!" exclaimed the owner of "Le Laconda". "In fact, zey are in my hotel, right now." he said. "What're you waiting for? GET EM!" yelled the King. Chaos ensued as people and soldiers ran in all directions, looking for the Daniels. "Okay, here's the plan" said Daniel 1. "I will get to the ticket master and get a ticket to Egypt. Daniel 2, look for an escape plan. Climb on top of this building and find a way to leave. Maybe we can take the King's carriage. Daniel 3, distract them. Yell at the people and soldiers, then run around and have them chase you as you run from roof to roof. Daniel 4, also help distract the people and the soldiers. Yell at them and they will be confused about which Daniel to go after. Let's go!" said Daniel 1. Just then, people started banging on the door. The hinges were popping loose as a huge crowd of people were trying to break through. Daniels stacked beds and chairs to the door. Daniel 1 climbed out of the windowsill and onto a small roof. He walked slowly around the roof. He climbed onto a bigger roof and walked faster. He saw a small shop that seemed to have tickets inside. There was no one inside. Daniel climbed down through a ladder and saw many tickets. He found one about Egypt. He looked through the timings and saw a boat leaving from Italy's southern port to Egypt. He checked the calendar. It was leaving today. He checked the clock. He had a few hours to get there. He took the ticket and left the bag of coins on the table. The ticket was 50 coins. Daniel 1 ran but stopped. He was cornered with angry villagers and soldiers surrounding him. They were closing in on him and he had no idea what to do. Just then Daniel 3 came to the rescue.

"HEY! YOU WANT ME! I HAVE THE WATCH". He pulled the broken watch out of his pocket. The crowd's attention was turned to Daniel 3 as he ran, from roof to roof. Daniel 4 joined in on the distraction. Daniel 2 ran up to Daniel 1. "Hey, you got the ticket?' asked Daniel 2." Yeah, got it!" said Daniel 1. "Awesome. I found the ride. We must take the king's chariot." said Daniel 2. They looked at the chariot. It was nearby, and the horses were standing there. Daniel 2 looked at the sky. "If the sun rises in the east and sets in the west, then that has to be south!" as Daniel 2 pointed towards the South. Daniel 3 and 4 were running from roof to roof. "Okay, let's go!" said Daniel 1. They ran towards the chariot and got in. Daniel 1 got in the front seat and was in control of the first horse. Daniel 2 will control the second horse. Daniel 3 and 4 noticed them and started running towards the chariot. They jumped off a small building and tumbled down a hill. They got into the chariot. "GO!" they yelled. The horses neighed and started galloping. Daniels struggled to hold on. The crowd of villagers and soldiers were running and following, angrily. The King was running even faster. "MY CHARIOT!" said the King. He ran fast and got at pace with the horses. The horses weren't going fast enough. Daniel 1 looked down from where he was sitting and saw the King right there. At any second, the King could jump on and take him down. The King was getting ready to attack. Danie 1 had to think fast. He reached down and grabbed the crown from the King. He put it on himself. The King lost focus and tripped and tumbled. The horses started accelerating and the crowd slowed down as the horses and the chariots accelerated. "WOO! WE DID IT!" said Daniels as they cheered. Daniel 1 rode proudly with the crown on him. After a few hours of travelling through the night, Daniel 1 could see a light in the faint distance. He smelled the seawater. "Okay y'all. We arrived!" he said. The Daniels cheered with excitement. They hopped off the carriage and fed the horses some apples from some trees. They walked up to the port and showed their tickets. The ticket master stared at them. "Ay, you can enter now." said the woman with a thick Italian accent. The Daniels walked onto the boat. They found a wooden table they could sit at. A waitress walked up to them and served them food and water. After a few minutes, the boat left. "Let me guide you to your room" said a waitress, kindly. She led them downstairs into the room. It was small and wooden, but cozy. It had 4 beds, a desk, a couch, and a closet to put clothes and shoes. It had a small window. On the other side of the window was water, and fish swam past. The Daniels thanked her and sat down. They looked out of the window a bit. "Alright. What's the plan?" said Daniel 1. "You know what I want?" said Daniel 2. "I want to get back in my timeline. Nothing against you guys, but I wish the timeline wasn't interrupted." he said. "You know, I don't think it's that good.

Let's say we fix the timeline and I go back to my part, where I'm supposed to jump off the building and glide safely like Daniel 1 did. Well, then I will be in the situation of Daniel 1. Then this whole situation will happen again, except I will experience it like Daniel 1. I am experiencing the mess up right now, then when the timeline is fixed and I go back to my part, it will mess up again, because now that the timeline is messed up, the event of us meeting each other is bound to happen right after gliding away from the castle. So, for all of us, except Daniel 1, this event will happen one more time for us and then we will be like Daniel 1. And then we can continue like Daniel 1 even though Daniel 1 only has to go through the event once." said Daniel 4. Everyone stared at him. "I have no idea what you just said. Let's just fix the timeline, and we will all be on our way." said Daniel 3. Days passed so similarly, just eating on the deck and watching the waves move and lounging around in the room. After a few days, a crazy storm came. Daniel looked out into the sky and saw dark clouds and thunder heading close. All the passengers went into their rooms. The Daniels locked their door. The ship started shaking violently. The waves were crashing against the ship, and it was moving up and down. Water started leaking into the room from the ceiling. Just then, a shark swam and banged into the glass window. It didn't break, but the glass cracked. Passengers were screaming as the boat kept rocking. Daniel could hear the thunder and the rain storming the boat. At that time, a wood plank from the wall broke in. Water started streaming in quickly. Within minutes, Daniels were ankle deep in water. "Lemme open the door" said Daniel 2. He grabbed the door handle, unlocked it, and shook it. "It's stuck." he said. "I have an idea. Push the furniture to the planks.". The Daniels pushed the desk to the plank. It slowed the water but didn't' stop it. After a few more minutes, the Daniels were hip deep in water. They started panicking now. Daniel 4 threw a book at a plank in the ceiling. The plank broke off and water started streaming in from the ceiling. After a few seconds, the window cracked open, and water started streaming in through the window. The Daniels were then shoulder deep in water. "Guys, come over here everyone! Let's break open more planks and swim to the surface." Daniel 2 broke open a few planks and water rushed in. He swam into the cold water and swam to the surface. The other Daniels followed. As they got to the surface, rain was colliding with the ocean. They could see the ship was sinking, and there were other people swimming as well. "Land!" yelled a passenger. Daniel glimpsed over and could see land, around a mile or 2 away. The Daniels swam as much as they could. After minutes and minutes of swimming, they finally got to the shore, cold and exhausted. They collapsed to the ground. They were so cold and tired and didn't realize when people grabbed them. They put them in a carriage and took them to a room. They were wrapped in cloths and layed down in a cozy room to sleep. They awoke the next day, feeling replenished and ready to find a way back home.

CHAPTER 10: HOROLOGY

Daniel 1 woke up, and he spoke. "Where are we?" he said. "As far as I know, the Egyptians took us from the beach and brought us to a room. They are great people." said Daniel 2. Just then, people walked in. They were speaking Arabic. "من أين أنت؟" said the guards. "واو، تبدون متشابهات" said the guards. "Uh, we don't understand the Egyptian dialect of Arabic. "What are you, Lebanese?" said a guard in an Arabic accent. "Yes" said Daniel 1s. "Okay, we know English, as you can tell. Well, are you guys' quadruplets? You look very very similar." said a guard. "Well, yes, not really, but I guess you could say that." said Daniel 4. "Okay. Well, your ship, eh, crashed. So, what can we help you with?" said the guard. "I'd like to speak to the creator of this watch." said Daniel 2. He took the watch out of his pocket. The guards were astonished. "Ze creator, waz..... long time ago. But I can take you to a watch master, horology, eh?" said a guard. "Sure" said Daniel 2. They got up and walked through the village. "Thank you for the help, by the way. You saved us from the storm." said Daniel 2. "God saved you. That was quite ze storm." said the guard. "Right, God saved us." said Daniel 2. They kept walking through the village until they arrived at a store. They walked in. A man sat in a room, tinkering on a watch. He turned around. "Hi, how can I help you?" he said. "We have a special watch." said Daniel 2. He showed him the watch. The watch master froze. "No... no way. What?" said the man. He looked around in confusion. "You, have it? The time travel watch?" he asked. The boys nodded. The man leaned forward. "Does it work?". "Yes". He smiled. "So …. you are from …. the future?" he asked. "Yes, 2022" said Daniel 1. "Great. GREAT!" he said. "Tell me, how did you find this? I've been searching for this my whole career." asked the man. "My … caretaker, Vespucci, gave it to me. Apparently, he found it in Beirut, Lebanon, 2022. I went on a plane and tried to get to California, but as the watch collided with objects, it would time travel me back hundreds to thousands of years ago. I am trying to get back to the future. As you can see, the people around me look like me. Well, they ARE me. We ran into each other as we time traveled. So, can you tell us how the watch works?" said Daniel 1. "Fascinating. I don't know how to get you back to your time, but I can get you to the creator." The man took the watch. He opened it up. "You see, if you open it up, and click this button, it takes you back to Ancient Egypt. Then, you can find the creator, named …. named …. Abilah, I believe. Ask him how to go back to your time. I wish you the best of luck." said the man. "Thank you so much." said Daniel 1. He ran outside of the store. He heard trumpets. He looked and saw a crowd of soldiers approaching, and what appeared to be King James in a chariot. "Attention, citizens, I am looking for Daniel. He has a golden watch that I want very much. Reward is $1,000,000 DOLLARS!!!!" yelled the King. "Quick, come here." said Daniel 1 to the rest of them. They got into a small room, held each other, and clicked the button. They were surrounded by dust. Once the dust settled, they realized they were in the same room, but it was instead made from hardened sand and clay. There were beautiful hieroglyphics on the wall. The Daniels were coughing. They went out of the room and looked around. The sun was beating down. There were people dressed in tunics. There were countless soldiers, carrying huge pillars of wood and blocks of sand. Carriages carried more blocks of sand. Daniel 1 suspected that they were going to build the famous pyramids of Egypt. He heard trumpets playing and saw a carriage being carried by horses. He saw a very young man, maybe a teenager, dressed in a gold tunic and surrounded by people. He was being treated by royalty. Daniel 1 assumed he had to be King Tut, because he was treated like a king and was so young. So, it did work. The watch brought them back in time. Over the course of a few hours, the Daniels went around and talked to people, asking if they knew the creator of the watch. No one understood them. They got some food and hopped in one of the carts carrying sand. Once they got to the pyramids, they were so amazed. There were thousands of people carrying huge blocks of sand, stacking them together, and sanding them together. So that's how the pyramids were built. No aliens, unfortunately. As they were walking around and looking around, they heard a man, frustrated, breaking something in his house. They walked over to the small tut made out of sand. "Excuse me, sir?" asked Daniel 1 as he walked in. The man turned around, holding a broken watch in his hand. He saw a blueprint that looked like it was for the time-travel watch. "Sorry for the disruption. My invention isn't working." he said. "The time-travel watch?" asked Daniel 2. He pulled the watch out of his pocket. The man jumped in joy. "Wait....wait.... it works?" he said, amazed. "Yes. We are from the year 2022. We need help getting back to the future." asked Daniel 1. "And you all look so similar. You must be the same people, but you ran into each other as the timeline messed up." said the man, walking around, fascinated. "Exactly. Could you help us?" asked Daniel 3. "Of course, I can." he said. He took the watch from Daniel 2. He looked at it and found a solution. "If you click this button, it will reset the timeline and take you back to your time period. But all of you will be put back in your time periods. So, you won't see each other again." said the man. They all looked at each other. "That's okay. We ARE each other. We will all be connected." They all hugged. "I've gotta give it to you, sir." said Daniel 4. "You are a genius." The man smiled. Glad to know my invention worked. And by the way, if you click that button, twice, it will take you to the time period you want to see the most.". said the man. "Okay, easy. If we click the button once, it takes us to Lebanon 2022. But if we click the button twice, it takes us to California 2022, the moment we hope to be at, to talk to Mike. That's what got us here, anyways." said Daniel 1. "Well, yes. Great meeting you all!!!!" said the man. They all said their goodbyes. They wished each other the best. "God bless you all. I never thought I'd become such good friends with...myself.... quite literally, but it's been great. You will make it back to the future. We will get through this. I love you, brothers! Good luck y'all, remember who we are doing this for. If we make it to the NBA, remember, all Glory to God. Gotta stay humble. Gotta track down Vespucci and bring him to America, of course. Remember, you're not only doing this for a better life for yourselves, but also for a better life for the world. We got this." said Daniel 1. They all hugged each other and smiled. They grabbed the watch and threw it into the sky. It twinkled in front of the sun. Daniel 1 closed his eyes. He kept them closed for a few seconds and opened them. He looked around, and saw he was on a dark, poorly lit street. He could see and hear the rain pattering on the ground. There was thunder in the distance. Daniel felt himself getting wet. He knew that his watch was set up to take him to the place he wanted to be the most, which was California. When Daniel looked around, he saw many signs and billboards in Arabic. He realized that he's probably not in California. He walked down a sidewalk and saw a familiar area. It was the area of land where Daniel had been raised by Vespucci. This means that Daniel was in Lebanon. For some reason, Lebanon was the place he wanted to be the most, but he didn't understand why yet. The watch had to have taken him back for a reason. Daniel decided to try time-traveling again, so he looked for the watch. As he looked around, he saw a couple whining, holding a box. There was a baby in the box, cooing. Daniel looked at the couple. They turned around. "Inta neeh?" they said in Arabic. There was a pause. "Are you okay?" asked the woman. Daniel responded. "Yes, thanks for asking.". The couple looked around a little bit. "Well, nice talking to you.". said the woman. They walked towards the patch of grass. Daniel walked towards them. The woman was crying. "It's ok. We can't take care of the baby. This is what's best for the baby." said the man. Daniel walked closer. "What are we going to name him? I have to add his name to the letter so people will know." said the man. The woman looked up at the sky. "Let's name him Daniel." she said. Daniel stopped. He couldn't believe what he was seeing. "I love you." they said. The couple kissed the baby, placed down the box, and walked away. A few moments later, Daniel saw a man walk out of a tent on the grass. He picked up the baby and hugged him. He realized it was Vespucci. And then it all made sense.

CHAPTER 11: THE TRUTH

Daniel was in Lebanon for a reason. He was time traveled to when his parents abandoned him and left him for Vespucci. This means the time he wanted to see the most was why his parents left him. He stood and looked out at the sky as thunder clapped in the background. He didn't understand why. He didn't understand why life was like that. He reached into his pocket and pulled out the watch. He threw it into the sky.

Daniel awoke. He was sitting in a plane. It looked familiar. As he got up and walked, he noticed something. He noticed himself sitting on the plane, holding the watch. He remembered that moment. He had traveled to the time where he was going on the plane and had crashed, and time traveled to 1492. He was now where the time travelling all started. Daniel easily could've taken the watch from the other Daniel and stopped the time travelling from stopping. However, he decided not to. He realized he went through so much, and learned so much, and became inspired and ready for his life. He went to the back room of the plane and put on a parachute. He sat by the door and waited. He felt the plane shake as the engines exploded. The plane started beeping and flying closer to the ground. Daniel pushed open the door and jumped out. He felt the wind blowing as he pulled his parachute and started gliding through the trees and mountains. He looked at the plane and saw it crash into the trees. He saw something sparkling, maybe the watch as it teleported the other Daniel to 1492. Daniel stopped at a mountain. It was cold and snowy. He descended as quickly and carefully as he could. He looked around for a moment and took some deep breaths. After a while, he started walking.

Eventually, Daniel arrived at the airport. He ran to one of the officials there and told them about the plane crash, and how Daniel escaped. The officials thanked him and sent teams into the forests to look for the plane crash and possible survivors. Daniel walked into the airport. A lot of people were looking at him weirdly. Daniel looked like he had gone through rough travels for the past few days, which is true. He literally traveled the world through time. He realized that the watch had to be a blessing in disguise. He checked the airport screens and saw that there was a flight to California from Philadelphia Airport. Daniel made it to the area and walked to the plane easily. It was easy for him to be young, since people probably assumed he was going to sit with his parents inside the plane. Daniel found an open seat and sat there. After a few minutes, the plane took off. Daniel looked outside as the airplane rose, and he saw all the buildings and lights. He saw mountains and nature as the plane flew more into the air. He took a nap and awoke a few hours later. He looked outside and saw beaches, and many buildings and houses in a huge city. He saw the famous Chase Center, which is where the Golden State Warriors played. He saw a huge banner on the front of the arena, with the famous Michael Johnson making the game winner for the NBA Championship back in 2022. Daniel had finally arrived at his destination and was on his way to meet Michael Johnson. He embarked on the long and stressful journey in order to meet Mike, anyways. He wanted to look for inspiration from him. Both Daniel and Mike had gone through rough lives and travels, and Daniel really looked forward to that. In fact, Daniel felt like he had gone through more. He used to be homeless in Lebanon, and got on a plane, and somehow time traveled through major events in human history, and survived, and finally made it to California. However, he still has a long way to go before he can achieve his dreams. He still trusted the Lord that one day, all his work would pay off. The plane landed soon after, and Daniel quickly prayed and got off the plane. Once he got into Los Angeles Airport, he didn't really know where to go from there. He didn't have money or a home to go to yet. All he had was the Man Above. He walked around without much of a goal. He decided to walk up to one of the restaurants inside the airport.

"Excuse me, I haven't seen my family for days, and I just found refuge in California, is it fine if I could have a free meal, please? I could do a favor to cover the cost of the meal if that's fine." asked Daniel. The restaurant owner looked at him favorably. He could see the dirt on Daniel and realized his story was probably true. He smiled. "Sure. Come inside, let's choose a meal." said the restaurant owner. Daniel cheered and thanked him. He chose to eat a Shrimp Lo Mein meal with water and ate it with passion. He was full and thankful. He didn't even have to do a favor for the meal. It was completely free. Daniel left the restaurant happy. He looked outside and saw that the sun was setting. It was beautiful. He checked the time on one of the airport screens, and it was almost 8:00 P.M. He decided he would sleep in the airport for the night and go to the arena the next day. He saw on TV screens in restaurants that the Warriors were playing the Lakers in Game 1 of the First Round of the NBA Playoffs. Daniel decided he would take the chance and go to the arena and try to meet Mike for a chance for glory.

CHAPTER 12: FOLLOWING THE FOOTSTEPS

Daniel awoke a few hours later. The morning sun was shining through the airport. He got up and walked to the water fountain, got refreshed, and walked to the airport exit. He grabbed a travel brochure to help guide himself to the arena. As he stepped out into the air of Los Angeles, he could hear the traffic and see the cars as the city of Los Angeles was very busy with people. Daniel stepped out and walked to a hill. He climbed up and got a great view of Los Angeles. He could see the Hollywood Sign in the distance. He could see Chase Center, which was his destination. The game would start in a few hours. Daniel finally made it. He still had work to do, but he finally made it. Daniel stepped down from the hill and walked towards the city. After a few minutes, Daniel arrived. Many people still gave him weird looks, because Daniel was practically wearing rags after his adventures time traveling. He checked his pockets and saw that he still had the time travel watch and could use it to escape just in case anything went wrong. As he walked through the city, he noticed how beautiful it was. He saw the Hollywood Walk of

Fame and saw the stars with the names of famous people. He knew one day his name would be on one of those stars. As Daniel walked through the crowds, he noticed he was hungry. He walked up to several restaurants and asked for free food and described what he went through, but many didn't offer help. Eventually, Daniel found a soup kitchen that was offering free food. After Daniel left, he kept going on his travels. Eventually, he arrived at the arena. It was around noon. Daniel had no idea how he could get inside the arena. He had to find a way. He walked around the arena and saw an area where NBA players and NBA coaching staff would drive into the arena. He looked around and saw ladders leading to the top of the arena with construction workers surrounding the area. Daniel sneaked around the parking lot and saw the security staff and construction workers talking to some of the NBA players. Daniel sprinted through the cars to the ladders. Luckily, no one noticed. He looked up and decided to climb up the ladders. He climbed hastily and got up to the top of the arena. He walked around the area and looked over the city of Los Angeles. It was beautiful as he saw the modern cars, the modern buildings, and the beautiful mountains and beaches surrounding the area. However, Daniel had to stay focused on his task. To sneak into the NBA game. He looked around and saw that the construction workers and security staff were still talking to the NBA players. Daniel looked and saw an open vent that led to vents that went indoors. Yes, he had to crawl around vents like they do in the movies, but that was one of his only options. Daniel got down into the vent and started crawling through the vents. He was surprised how much room there was. As Daniel crawled, he looked down at some of the open vents and saw people entering the arena to watch the NBA game. Daniel kept crawling until he had to go left or right. He decided to go right, because it has to be the right way, get it? He kept going for minutes until he saw another vent he could look through. He looked down and saw what looked like a locker room. There were jerseys, chairs, shoes, water bottles, and more in the locker room. Daniel decided he could enter the arena from there. He pushed open the vent and prepared to jump out. He saw a pile of jerseys that he could land on. He jumped out of the vent onto the jerseys, which were surprisingly soft. Daniel got up and heard the crowd roaring. Daniel got out of the locker room quickly. He ran out into the hallways and sneaked around people. He followed the sound of the fans which got louder and louder as he got closer and closer. Eventually, he found a huge entrance where the players would enter. Daniel sprinted through the entrance and looked out onto the huge and energetic crowds in the stadium. Daniel cheered and jumped in joy. He finally made it. He was so happy. He ran over to the sideline and found a free seat. Daniel was extremely blessed to find a courtside seat, and no one even questioned if he had tickets. Daniel sat down and looked around the court. He saw his inspiration, Mike Johnson. He watched as Mike dribbled, crossed LeBron James, and made a three. The crowd roared. Daniel watched in pure joy. The game kept going back and forth, and the energy in the arena was definitely at its maximum peak.

CHAPTER 13: INSPIRATION

The game was soon in the fourth quarter. Daniel was surrounded by many celebrities with front court seats. Daniel realized he was sitting next to Jennifer Lopez, Kevin Hart, Dwyane Johnson, and Shakira. They were cheering a lot as the Warriors kept scoring clutch points. Mike drove in and got his first posterizer on Anthony Davis. The crowd jumped up and roared. Mike had gotten his first dunk, and it was amazing. Daniel was jumping up and cheering. As Mike was jumping up and hyping up the crowd, he made eye contact with Daniel. Mike and Daniel stared at each other. Mike pointed at him and ran back up the court. Daniel sat back down. He didn't know what had just happened, but Daniel felt like he understood Mike. He felt like Mike understood him. Daniel watched as 1 minute was left on the clock. The Warriors were down by 10. Draymond Green blocked Anthony Davis. Klay Thompson grabbed the rebound and dribbled up the court and made a quick 3. 50 seconds remained with the Warriors down 7. LeBron James inbounded the ball to Malik Monk but was quickly stolen by Curry. He shot a 3 from deep, was fouled, and made it! "AND 1!" the crowd shouted. Daniel and the celebrities were jumping up and down in happiness. Jennifer Lopez, Kevin Hart, Dwyane Johnson, and Shakira were all jumping around and cheering. The started jumping around with Daniel and Daniel was cheering with joy. Steph Curry scored the free throw. 38 seconds remained with the Warriors down 3. The Warriors could definitely win the game now. A timeout was called by the Los Angeles Lakers. After the timeout, Curry inbounded the ball to Johnson at the sidelines. Mike stood there, with the ball as he looked over the court. Michael Johnson stared at LeBron James as he was guarding him. Mike took deep breaths. He pulled up from deep. The 3 goes in. "TIE GAME!" yells the announcers. The crowd was roaring at its most so far. Mike was amazed. Mike waited 20 seconds and pulled up from near half court to tie the game. 18 seconds remained in the game. The Lakers inbounded the ball. Malik Monk passed the ball to Talen-Horton Tucker. He passed the ball to Anthony Davis. He passed the ball to Dwight Howard. He passed the ball to LeBron James. LeBron waited, and then drove in for a powerful dunk. The Lakers led by 2 with 10 seconds remaining. The Golden State Warriors called a timeout. As Daniel was watching the game happen, he realized this game was very similar to game 7 of the Warriors V.S. Cavaliers

NBA Championship where the Warriors had won the 2022 NBA Championship. Even though it was only game 1 of the first round of the NBA playoffs, Daniel knew it was going to be an amazing game. The crowd and the players definitely agreed.

CHAPTER 14: NEW BEGINNINGS

Daniel sat back down as the Warriors timeout ended. Steph Curry inbounded the ball to Mike Johnson. During the 2022 playoffs, the Warriors didn't trust Mike. During the 2023 playoffs, the Warriors definitely trusted Mike as he was the scoring champ, the NBA MVP and DPOY and had done so much for the Golden State Warriors and the NBA. Mike dribbled up the court. 10 seconds remained. The crowd was chanting the time countdown as Mike dribbled and looked LeBron James in the eye. 5 seconds remained. Michael Johnson stepped back for 3. The crowd was quiet. The buzzer goes off. The 3 goes in the basket.

The stadium erupts in cheers.

Daniel was jumping around as confetti flew everywhere and everyone was cheering and dancing. Daniel found himself in a huge crowd of celebrities, fans, and players. He bumped into LeBron James. He looked at him. Daniel smiled. He finally made it to where he wanted to be. He was crowded with people around him celebrating the Golden State Warriors win. Daniel ran around the court looking for Mike. He finally saw him. Daniel sprinted over to Mike. "Yo my man Mike Johnson, lemme tell you something. I come from Lebanon, and I traveled across the world just to see you because you inspire me. I read about your stories of how you went from being stranded across the world to becoming one of the best NBA players right now! Please give me some advice, man, I would really appreciate it. I want to succeed like you do!" said Daniel with enthusiasm. Mike stared at him. "Yeah man. Glad I could motivate you." said Mike. Daniel smiled. "So, what tips do you have?". Mike looked at him. He nodded and walked away. Daniel wondered why he was acting so weird. Daniel thought that Mike would be happy to mentor someone who had been through a lot, like Mike had. Daniel was standing around on the court when he noticed Mike talking to security guards, pointing at him. Daniel got scared when the guards started running towards him. Mike ratted him out! How did Mike find out he didn't have tickets? Daniel began running through crowds of people. He sprinted back to the Warriors locker room as fast as he could. He ran in and grabbed a chair and climbed back up into the vent as NBA players and coaches stared at him in confusion. Daniel crawled through the vents as fast as he could. He could hear the security guards running and yelling for Daniel. He kept crawling through the vents until he reached another opening in the vents. He heard creaking. Daniel stayed still. Then the vents collapsed. Daniel fell from the vents onto the main floor of the NBA stadium. Daniel got up coughing. Two security guards sprinted to him and grabbed him. Mike walked up to Daniel. "How....how did you know I didn't have a ticket?" asked Daniel in desperation. "I saw you didn't have the courtside wristbands." said Mike. They shared an awkward silence. "I....I thought you would understand me. We both went through a lot and just want to succeed. I thought.... I thought you would help me." asked Daniel. Mike stopped. "I don't." Mike turned and walked away. Daniel sat in silence as the security guards carried him to a truck. They threw him into the back of a van and began driving. "Where ya from, son?" asked a security guard. "Lebanon." said Daniel quietly. Daniel didn't understand why Mike betrayed him like that. And why was Daniel being sent away for sneaking into an NBA game? Daniel felt like that was too much. Daniel was probably going to be thrown away to some random island. Just for sneaking into an NBA game to find a better chance at becoming successful. Daniel felt hopeless until he had an idea. He could use the watch to maybe escape the truck hopefully. Daniel felt his pocket. "Of course," he said. The watch wasn't there. It must have fell out as he fell from the vents. Daniel layed down. He looked up at the ceiling of the truck. The truck shook as it drove over a hill and Daniel tumbled around the truck. After a while, he fell asleep.

CHAPTER 15: BETRAYED

Daniel was tired but he remembered a few events. He remembered guards picking him up from the truck into a building. He felt himself being put on a seat. He remembered being on a plane that flew off, for a while. Daniel woke up. He found himself in another truck, but it seemed more broken as the truck was rattling. Daniel overheard the guards speaking in what sounded like Arabic. Daniel looked outside a small window in the truck and saw lots of desert as the trucks drove up to a building with military people guarding it. They let the truck in. They drove for a few more minutes until the truck finally stopped. Daniel felt scared. Why was this happening to him? Because he just sneaked into an NBA game? Daniel was very angry at Mike. He was very angry. The guards opened the truck and grabbed Daniel out. They carried Daniel inside and Mike realized it was a prison. They threw him into a cell and shut the door. Daniel got up, yelling, asking why he was arrested. He asked for a lawyer. No one cared. After minutes of yelling,

Daniel stopped. He sat down on his dirty bed and looked outside the small window. He could hear people yelling in Arabic.

After a few hours, the guards went to Daniel. "Time to eat" said one guard. That guard went up to the cell and started unlocking it. Daniel stopped, because his voice sounded familiar. The guard even looked familiar. Very familiar. "Vespucci, hurry up" said one of the guards. Daniel froze. That was Vespucci! The man that had taken care of him for years. Daniel remembered, before his journey started, how Vespucci had been taken to the Lebanese military. Now, Daniel was probably in Lebanon, and Vespucci had seen him! He would surely be saved by Vespucci!

"Come on, boy," said Vespucci. Daniel was confused. Did Vespucci recognize him? "Vespucci....Vespucci? Do you remember me? It's Daniel!" he said. Vespucci stared at him. "No.... come on boy time to eat." said Vespucci. Daniel felt betrayed. How come Mike and Vespucci had to betray him like that? How come they were like that?

Daniel walked slowly to the lunchroom. He sat down and ate. He was surrounded by a lot of people, all chattering in Arabic. Daniel was alone at a table, eating food that didn't taste that good. After a few minutes, the people were released from the lunchroom back to their rooms. Daniel sat on the broken bed as the guards locked the doors. Daniel felt like that was too much. How could he be arrested and sent back to Lebanon for merely sneaking into an NBA game?

After hours of Daniel walking around his room and looking outside the window, Daniel fell asleep.

He woke up to the sound of people yelling outside. It was morning.

"Yo, uh, go to ze outside. You go play sports, okay?" said a guard in a thick, Arabic accent. Daniel got up. "Okay" he said as he walked outside. Daniel looked around and realized how broken down the prison was. The whole place was practically collapsing and was surrounded by a huge fence. Daniel walked over to the broken basketball hoop. He picked up the ball and started playing, even though he wasn't that good.

"Ay, bro, you hoop?" said one of the people outside. He walked over menacingly to Daniel. "Yeah." said Daniel. "Let's play," said the man. A lot of people came to the courts and formed a team. And then they started playing. Daniel didn't play well. The inmates were playing well against Daniel. They even started taunting him. Daniel yelled in frustration and ran around the courts. "I DON'T BELONG HERE!" "I DIDN'T DO ANYTHING WRONG!" yelled Daniel with frustration. The guards ran in and grabbed Daniel and put him back into a room. Danie started grabbing the gate and shaking it. Dust was collecting. Daniel then remembered how he used to be trapped in the king's castle and was able to escape by shaking the gate open. Daniel decided to try that. He shook the gate for 10 minutes, but it was sturdier, so it didn't move much. Daniel sat down on his bed and fell asleep. He woke up. He ate. He played basketball. He steadily improved. He fell asleep. He woke up. He played basketball. He steadily improved. Days turned into weeks, and weeks turned into months. After a while, Daniel was detained for 2 months. It had gone by so fast. As Daniel was walking to the lunchroom, he saw something on the TV. He saw how the NBA Finals were two days away. Daniel remembered going to Game 1 of the First Round of the NBA Playoffs in April. Now it was June, and Game 7 of the NBA Finals was happening. It was the Golden State Warriors V.S. the Brooklyn Nets, and whoever wins Game 7 becomes NBA champions. It was in Chase Center in Los Angeles, California. Daniel didn't like Mike after what he did to him, but he was still proud that Mike had helped his team through the playoffs to face the Nets. Both teams were playing great, and this definitely would be a great game. And then, Daniel had an idea.

CHAPTER 16: PILOT

Daniel decided it was time for him to escape the prison. It would be hard, but his life was practically already an adventure movie, so he decided to do it. He looked around the yard and saw a plane right outside. It looked like it worked, because Daniel saw guards flying the plane around. Daniel decided he had to start a riot as a distraction and somehow get over the fence, get into the plane, and fly to California for another chance to get Daniel's attention.

Daniel had a lot to do. First, he had to get the key for the plane. He also had to get a phone to use as a GPS. Daniel sneaked around the yard until he spotted the room of the warden. Daniel hid behind a bush and looked into the room. He saw the warden on her computer. Daniel hummed a buzzing sound to make the warden think they got notifications. The warden fell for the trick and picked up her phone. Daniel looked closely and saw the password the warden entered. "1,2,3,4,5,6" thought Daniel. What an easy password. Next, Daniel had to start a riot to get the warden out of his office in order to take the phone and the key. Daniel saw the key on the Wardens keychain around his belt. Daniel ran over to the side of the building and saw a huge alarm. Daniel pulled the alarm. Immediately, people ran out of the room. Daniel yelled "TIME TO ESCAPE!" loudly. The inmates started cheering and running around the courtyard. It was chaos. The guards were running around trying to detain them, but the inmates were going crazy and trying to crawl over the wall. Daniel saw the warden on the other side of the yard. Daniel sprinted over to the warden and snatched the key from her keychain. She yelled and started chasing him. Daniel dashed away and into the office areas. Daniel sprinted until he saw the warden's office. He ran in and took her phone from her desk. He sprinted outside. He found himself trapped in a corner with the warden coming up to him. Daniel ran to the right. So did the warden. Daniel sprinted to the left. The warden got juked and slid to the floor. The inmates started cheering. Daniel yelled in joy and sprinted towards the fence to escape. Daniel could see helicopters and tanks approaching in the distance. As Daniel got closer to the fence, the inmates started climbing on top of each other, in order to make a way for Daniel to get over the fence easier. Daniel climbed on top of the people. He jumped and grabbed to the top of the fence. He climbed himself up. He cheered. The inmates cheered too. Daniel looked down. He saw the fence was partly slanted. Daniel climbed down and slid down the fence. He got down safely. He ran over to the plane. As he got closer, he felt someone grab him. "I gotchu" said the guard. Daniel groaned. His escape wasn't working. Daniel looked at the guard. It was Vespucci. "Wait...." said Vespucci. He let go of Daniel. "Are you …. Daniel?!" said Vespucci. Daniel smiled. "Yes! YES!" said Daniel with joy. Vespucci finally recognized him. "I didn't recognize you until now because you look so different." said Vespucci. "I know, a lot's happened. I'm trying to escape back to the NBA game. I was taken here for sneaking into the NBA game, and now I'm going back for another chance to go the NBA game." said Daniel. Vespucci smiled. "I believe in you. We will meet soon." said Vespucci, with hope. He handed Daniel a paper. "This is my phone number. Contact me when you make it." said Vespucci. Daniel replied, "I will. I WILL!" with excitement. "Now go, make me proud. God be with you!" said Vespucci. "God be with you too!" said Daniel. He hugged Vespucci and sprinted to the plane. He put in the keys and turned the plane on. He unlocked the phone and searched for the destination for California. He found the location. Daniel had no idea how to fly a plane. He grabbed the stick and pulled it down. The plane started moving forward. "PLEASE LEAVE THE VEHICLE IMMEDIATELY!" said the army in speakerphones. Daniel pulled down the lever. The plane started going up. "FIRE!" yelled the army from the speakerphones. Daniel saw tanks firing bombs at the planes. The army started shooting at the planes. Daniel grabbed the steering wheel and flew higher and flew around the missiles. He flew up and turned around and flew over the yard and flew away. He saw helicopters and planes flying close to him. Daniel clicked a button on the plane, and it zoomed faster. The helicopters began shooting at the plane. Daniel was freaking out. He couldn't believe he was driving a military plane. However, he had to escape and get to California as soon as possible. He zoomed up and flew around a cloud. After many minutes of flying around clouds and flying in many directions, Daniel finally lost the helicopters. He was flying free. He looked down from the plane and saw the blue ocean for miles. Daniel got up and checked his GPS. He just had to keep going forward. Daniel set the military plane on autopilot and relaxed for a few hours. Soon Daniel saw land after hours of travelling in the plane. As he flew more and more, he could see houses and buildings. His GPS told him to keep going forward.

Daniel kept flying the plane for a few more hours until, eventually, he reached his destination. As he flew, he could see the Hollywood sign, Chase Center, and more. Now, Daniel had to land. He flew near a nearby airport and started descending. He pulled the lever back as he got closer to the runway and clicked the parking button. The plane slowed down as the wheels drove the plane forward. Daniel stopped the plane and parked it. He clicked a button and the door of the plane opened. Daniel took the phone and left the plane. He was surprised how easy it was for him to fly the plane and land it. As Daniel walked away, he noticed something on the plane. There was a small device attached to the plane, and it was flashing lights. Daniel then heard planes flying in the distance. He looked up and saw several army planes flying towards him. Daniel realized that device had to be a tracker, and the military found him that way. Daniel saw the military planes land in the distance, and multiple soldiers sprinted out of the plane towards Daniel. He yelled and sprinted away. He ran towards Chase Center in the distance, and he had to take a shortcut into a forest to get there faster. Daniel ran into the forest. He was hopping over sticks, running around trees, and he could hear the soldiers right behind him. He heard bullets whizzing past him. Daniel prayed to God and kept running. Daniel ran towards a hill and tumbled down another hill to get towards Chase Center. He finally got out of the forest and started running down towards the city. The soldiers followed him and ran after him. Daniel slid down another hill and sprinted towards Chase Center. He ran through streets, hopped onto cars, and ran through many buildings. After sprinting a while, he finally got there. He got to the entrance but didn't know where to go. He looked behind him and saw the soldiers running close behind. He had no idea what to do.

CHAPTER 17: FRIENDSHIP

Daniel ran towards the main entrance of the arena. The soldiers yelling distracted the security guards so Daniel was able to get into the arena quickly and efficiently. Daniel ran in and made it to the court. The court was packed with people cheering. Daniel ran down the stairs until he made it to the front court. He was sweating. He saw security guards running to him. They grabbed him. "Hey, hey, leave bro alone!" said a familiar voice. Daniel realized it was Dwayne Johnson. "He's with me," said Dwayne. The security guards let me go. "Thank you so much, Dwyane. Why'd you help me?" asked Daniel. "I realized you just wanted a chance to improve your life. You seem like a great person, so I want to help you out. Let's watch this game" said Dwayne, smiling. Daniel thanked him and sat down. He watched the game go by. Daniel was so fascinated by the amazing basketball. He watched Mike hesi, step back, and make an insane 3 from deep. He watched Russell Westbrook lob the ball to LeBron for a windmill dunk. He watched Curry spin into a wide open three. He watched LeBron make a 3 from halfcourt. He watched Johnson drive into the lane for an amazing dunk. And soon, it was the fourth quarter. The game was tied, 140-140.

CHAPTER 18: SECOND CHANCE

Daniel watched as the fourth quarter began. It started off with Klay Thompson and Stephen Curry making amazing threes. LeBron James and Russell Westbrook responded with threes of their own. The game went back and forth for the majority of the fourth quarter. Then, with 1 minute remaining, LeBron James made a deep 3. He rebounded the ball and drove in for a powerful dunk. The Lakers were up 5. A timeout was called. Right after the timeout, the ball was inbounded to Mike at halfcourt. He stood there with the ball, staring at LeBron. The shot clock was going. Mike took the 3 from halfcourt. Swish. The crowd erupted in cheers as Mike made the 3 with 20 seconds left in the NBA Championship Game 7. This was such a similar scenario to the Warriors V.S. Cavaliers NBA Championship Game 7 where Mike made the clutch game winner for the NBA Championships. The Warriors called another timeout.

Daniel was sweating. He was so nervous about who would win the game. He was staring at Mike for a while. The timeout then ended. The Warriors and the Lakers walked back onto the court.

The clock starts going. Anthony Davis inbounds the ball to LeBron. He brings the ball up the court. LeBron hezis and shoots a midrange shot. Steph Curry rebounds the ball. He passes it to Michael Johnson. 10 seconds remain. Daniel stands up and eagerly watches Mike dribble the ball, guarded by LeBron James. The Warriors are down 2. There are 5 seconds left. Daniel steps back. He shoots the 3. The clock buzzes.

The shot goes in. The crowd erupts in cheers as Michael Johnson makes the game winner to bring the Warriors up 1. The Warriors win Game 7 of the NBA Finals and are the 2022 NBA Champions!! Daniel is running onto the court, cheering and jumping in joy. Fans are running onto the court and confetti is flying everywhere. Everyone is cheering in happiness. Daniel is running around, talking to celebrities, when he sees Mike. They look at each other. "CONGRATULATIONS ON YOUR GAME WINNER! YOU ARE SUCH AN INSPIRATIONAL PLAYER AND YOU HAVE DONE SO MUCH GREAT JOB IM PROUD OF YOU!" yelled Daniel to Mike. "Wait, it's you!" said Mike, smiling. "Yeah man. I don't know why you tried to get me away from the NBA game. I'm back to the NBA game, and I'd like some inspiration bro. You helped the Warriors win another championship! I also want to succeed in life, and I need some advice bro!" said Daniel. Mike looked at him. "Meet me in the media room. We will talk soon." Mike went and celebrated with his teammates. Daniel smiled and sat down at his seat. He looked around at the fans cheering, and the Warriors accepting the NBA championships trophies. Daniel gets up and starts cheering. He was proud of himself for making it to the NBA, and now he has a chance to talk to Daniel. He was so happy. Daniel thanked God for all his blessings and started walking over to the media room. He sat down in a seat and watched as Mike gave an amazingly inspirational speech. "You know, it's been a tough journey here. However, here we are, with NBA Championships! I want to thank my family, my coaches, my teammates, the fans, and most importantly God. It's been a long but rewarding journey, and I'm glad my career is starting off greatly. I've been through a lot, and I want to tell you, if you work really, really hard, trust the Lord, and never, never give up, I promise you that you WILL achieve your dreams. YOU WILL ACHIEVE YOUR DREAMS!" said Mike enthusiastically. His teammates started jumping and cheering in the media room. Daniel got up and applauded along with other people in the room. Mike walked over to Daniel and sat down next to him.

"Tell me everything." said Mike.

CHAPTER 19: SAVED

Vespucci sat in the chair, looking at the TV. He smiled as he saw the Warriors celebrating their 2022 NBA Championship win. He saw Daniel on the court, jumping and cheering too with celebrities and NBA players surrounded by him. Vespucci got up and yelled in happiness. "HE MADE IT! HE MADE IT!" said Vespucci. He was so proud how Daniel made it back to the NBA games and would have a chance to talk to Mike. Just then, the TV switched to an emergency broadcast. Vespucci got up and looked at the TV as other guards came near to see what was going on.

"This just in, the Republic of Canada has officially declared war on Romania. This marks the beginning of World War 3. Canada is beginning with an attempt to takeover the Middle East. It is being seen that the Canadian army is arriving at the front of Lebanon to take over the Middle East. The U.S.A. is sending emergency troops currently to aid the Middle East, but they must act quick. Please stay safe, and good luck to all." said the newsperson.

Vespucci stood in shock, still staring at the TV. Just then, a huge rumble shook the whole building. Vespucci fell and saw parts of the ceiling collapsing with dust flying everywhere. The alarms started blazing as guards started running outside. He saw guards getting into their tanks and helicopters. Vespucci ran to the entrance and saw thousands of troops marching, with huge tanks and planes flying above. He saw a huge plane drop a missile. Vespucci screamed. He sprinted towards the building. The missile collided with the ground. Vespucci flew forward into the building as the walls collapsed from the explosions. Inmates started running around in chaos. The Canadian army took all of the inmates and the guards and put them into huge trucks. One man walked over, grabbed Vespucci, and put him into a truck with other people. Vespucci looked outside as the courtyard exploded and the Candian army started moving forward.

Eventually, the army got to the Lebanese capital. The soldiers ran in and commanded the Lebanese president to give them control. The president was frightened and agreed. Canada signed an official deal to make Lebanon the Candian Republic of Lebanon. Vespucci watched from a television in the truck, which was still moving to somewhere he didn't know. He was frustrated as the Canadian army was taking over his home country. He couldn't believe World

War 3 was happening. He wished he could call Daniel and ask how he was doing. Someone has to stop Canda, thought Vespucci. Someone.

Vespucci glanced towards outside. He saw how the truck was still driving over deserts.

After a few hours, the truck arrived at this huge facility. All of the inmates and guards were taken out of the trucks and thrown into this huge building. They were each put into separate rooms. Vespucci wished he was never taken by the military. He wished he could just be with Daniel in Los Angeles, California. Vespucci felt sad, but he was happy that Daniel was succeeding.

Vespucci walked into the café to eat some food and watch TV. He sat down, next to many other people, and watched WW3 unfold.

"This just in, we have very important news. The Canadian Republic has officially taken multiple Middle Eastern countries, and in a few hours, will officially have taken over the entirety of the Middle East. It is reported there are battles raging on for control of Romania. The war started because Romania refused to give Canada control of the country, so Canada left NATO and wanted to take it over by force. Since Romania is a part of NATO, the United States and multiple other countries have joined in the battle to protect Romania. However, the Canadian army has all of the Middle Eastern armies in control and are using them to go against the NATO armies. It is quite strange how Canada, who used to be in NATO, is going against their former allies. In addition, Canada is attempting to gain full control of Russia. The capital is currently being stormed, and the leader of Canada, Chalito Varat, is demanding full control of Russia and its economy. We will have more in the next hour." said the newsperson, very seriously.

Vespucci sighed. How could the world come to this, he thought.

"I DEMAND CONTROL! I DEMAND IT" yelled Chalito Varat. He stared at Putin. "You want Russia? Take it!" said Putin, storming off. He was clearly intimidated by the power of Canada and the Middle East, which had been taken over by Canada. Chalito Varat signed multiple papers and made it official. Russia is now a part of the Canadian Republic.

For the next few days, Canada was taking full control of Asia. Canada first took countries like Kazakhstan and Uzbekistan, and then eventually took over major countries like China and Japan. At this point, Canada had insane amounts of power. Canada had officially taken all of Asia. Canda started its takeover of African countries. Canada then went and took control of several islands near Asia and took over Australia. They even took over Antarctica.

At this point, Canda becomes the most powerful government in world history. They had full control of the world, except for Europe and parts of North America. All these takeovers had happened in the past few days. Vespucci was still trapped in the building. He would wake up, go to the café to eat, and watched TV to see what countries had been taken over by Canada. Vespucci wished he could call Daniel. He didn't know how Daniel was doing. He hoped Daniel was okay. Daniel still has Vespucci's number, so hopefully, soon, Daniel could call Vespucci.

Within the next few days, the battle continued raging in Romania. While the world focus was mostly on defending Romania, Canada took over several powerful countries in Europe. Canada had full control of Europe, except for Romania. At this point, Canada was forcing all the Asian, African, European, Canadian, Australian, and more armies to go against the defenders of Amsterdam. The United States Armies and other armies in South America were struggling to defend against the rest of the world.

Vespucci turns on the TV.

"This just in, we have more news about Canada. Two weeks later, from WW3 being declared on Romania, it is official that Canada now has full control of the world. Canada took over all of South America by surprise, and took over the U.S.A., while it was distracted in Romania. The U.S.A was one of the most powerful countries, but now, Canada is in full control of the world's countries. The leader of Canada, Chalito Varat, wanted full control of the world's countries. Now, Canada has won the battle in Romania and now controls Romania. Canada vows to create a dictatorship and wants to control the world's economy. It really will take an amazing revolt to win back the world." said the newsperson.

Vespucci turned off the TV. He got up and went for a walk. He sat down and took some time to think. He thought for hours. He didn't know how to help the world. However, he had to try.

CHAPTER 20: REVOLUTION

Daniel finished his talk with Mike. "Great talk, bro. I shouldn't have sent you off to Lebanon. Now, let me help you out. I want to get my agent to also help manage you. I'll call him and have him set up an apartment nearby for you to live. We can start working on plans to improve your future and find success!" said Mike, enthusiastically. Daniel thanked him. He was guided into a limousine by the agent and was taken to a nice apartment overviewing Los Angeles. Daniel was given the house keys and a new iPhone, and he entered the apartment. It was beautiful. Daniel sat down on the bed and looked over Los Angeles at night. He looked at all the twinkling lights in the city. He felt happy that he finally made it. He took a long shower, ate lots of food, drank lots of water, and went and sat in the living room. He read the Holy Bible and picked up his phone to call Vespucci. He wanted to let him know that he made it, and he wanted to get Vespucci to Los Angeles. He called Vespucci multiple times, but he didn't answer. Daniel called him again, and someone actually picked up. It was quiet for a few seconds. "Hello?" said a man, with a deep voice. "Vespucci?" asked Daniel. He sounded differently. "No." said the man. He ended the call. Daniel was extremely confused. Did Vespucci give him the wrong number? Did someone take Vespucci's phone? Daniel grabbed the TV remote and turned on the TV. He went to the news channel to see what was going on. When he saw the news, he couldn't believe his eyes.

"This just in, Canada has officially signed deals to have full control of the United States. This now puts the Republic of Canada in full control of all countries in the world. There are no longer hundreds of countries, all land in the world is now taken over by Republic of Canada. It all started when Canada declared war on Romania to use its economy. Since Romania is a part of NATO, other countries had to get involved to defend Romania, which started WW3. Canada had been very strategic and had started off by taking over Lebanon, as you can see here." said the newsperson.

Daniel watched the TV, and saw the Lebanese army being taken and forced into buildings. He saw Vespucci being taken into the building as well. Daniel didn't know what to do. He had to find a way to help.

"Canada has used the militaries it has taken over to take over other countries. Well, now Canada is in full control. Something MUST be done to save the world. I wish you all the best. God Bless." said the newsperson.

Daniel turned off the TV.

He sat down on a chair and looked outside at the city of Los Angeles for a long while. He looked down on his phone and saw all of the news notifications talking about Canada's takeover of the world.

How was this even possible? Daniel just couldn't believe the way his life had been going. For years he had been in Lebanon with Vespucci and had found his way to America for a better life. Somehow, he experienced time traveling, met many people and escaped to get to the present time and went back to California. He got to the NBA games, was sent back to Lebanon, and still got back to the NBA games. He finally got his life settled, which was one of his major goals in going to America, but now he was watching as the world was being taken over by the Republic of Canada. His life didn't feel real, but it was. It was real. Daniel picked up his phone and called Mike. "We have to talk. Meet me tomorrow for breakfast at Chase Center." said Daniel. He put his phone down and went to sleep.

After a few hours, Daniel was waken up by the loud whirring of helicopters. Daniel looked outside and saw multiple helicopters flying over Los Angeles, and many soldiers were dropping out of them onto the ground. They were scouting out the area and taking over control of Los Angeles. The Candian Republic had been doing this with many other major cities worldwide, as Daniel saw on the news. Daniel was scared, but he didn't know what to do. Not yet. He trudged back to his bed and fell asleep.

Daniel awoke the next morning. He showered, brushed his teeth, changed his clothes, drank some water, and went down the elevator to the lobby of the apartment. He went outside and began walking to Chase Center. He kept trying to respond to Vespucci, but no one responded. As Daniel was walking, he felt like Los Angeles was different. It wasn't bustling with the same energy as it usually does. There were fewer cars and fewer people around. It was like lots of the population left to other places. As Daniel was walking, he was stopped by a soldier. The soldier held him still while another soldier patted him down. Daniel was freaking out and stayed as still as he could. The soldiers let him go. As Daniel walked to Chase Center, he didn't feel safe. He saw many soldiers watching him and other people from places around Los Angeles. He didn't like the way he was being monitored. He looked around and saw how many businesses had been closed by the soldiers. He saw some soldiers boarding up some businesses on the other side of Chase Center. Daniel didn't know what was going on, or why.

He kept walking towards Chase Center. Daniel saw military trucks driving around. As Daniel got closer to Chase Center, he also saw the airport. It was absolutely packed. There were hundreds, thousands of cars trying to get into the airport. There were so many people entering the airport. There were many military people going there to monitor the travels. Daniel looked away and took deep breaths. He thought about how his other versions of himself, Daniel 2,3, and 4, were doing. He probably expected they were going through the same things as he was going through.

"Daniel! Over here!" said Mike. Daniel looked over and jogged to Mike. "How's it going man. What do you want to talk about?" asked Mike. "This is important." said Daniel. They sat down in one of the breakfast restaurants near Chase Center. "Did you see the news?" asked Daniel. Mike nodded. "We have to do something." said Daniel. "Exactly. I was thinking the same thing." said Mike. "Look what I found. It's a website that tracks where the Candian Republic is centered in. They have military setpoints across major cities in the world, but they are mainly set up in New York City. The Candian Republic took full control of the city, and everyone evacuated the city so far. Apparently, the leader, Chalito Varat, wants full control of the economy. He wants to bring glory to Canda by taking over the world, which is cliche but has to be stopped. See these prices of items on Amazon right now." said Daniel. He showed Mike how iPhones costs had skyrocketed from hundreds to thousands of dollars to millions of dollars. "Now, not many people would be able to afford everyday items. He increased the prices of things like napkins to $10,00 and more! Now look at this ad he made.

"Hello, citizens of Earth, this is Chalito Varat." said Varat, in a thick accent. "I know you see the crazy prices I have made. However, if you want to get prices back to normal, each human on Earth must donate 50% of the money they have! Or else, the prices will keep increasing." Chalito then shows as he increases the price of an iPhone 12 from $1 million to $1 billion. "Hahahahahahahahaha!" says Chalito. "Donate now from the link, thanks!" said Chalito.

Mike checked the link on his computer. "Look, people worldwide have donated $10 billion dollars so far. He is so greedy. This money should go towards charities instead." said Mike, angrily. "I feel you, bro. It's just... it doesn't feel right. Now, I have a plan," said Daniel. Mike listened eagerly. "We have to get to New York City, and we have to revolt. We need to get as many people as possible to get into the Candian Republics main building, then we demand Chalito Varat to let the world be free again. And then, we are free from Canda's control!" said Daniel. "Great plan. We just need to know how to get people to know." said Mike.

"I have ideas. Step 1: we have to get the word out. We post videos on social media, we post signs around cities, we appear on television shows, we make advertisements, and more. Once the world knows what to do, we move on to the next step. Step 2: we ask airplane companies around the world to provide free flights to all willing supporters to arrive at New York City. Step 3: We gather all the people to revolt at the headquarters and get into the headquarters to show Chalito Varat that we want freedom. And then Step 4: Chalito gives us freedom." said Daniel. "Great plan," said Mike. "I'm gonna call the agent and let him know about everything," said Mike. "Great idea. We can start with social media posts." said Daniel. Mike had over 100 million followers on both Instagram and TikTok, and over 30 million YouTube subscribers. He gave Daniel shoutouts and got Daniel to a decent 10 million followers on both Instagram and TikTok, and 5 million subscribers on YouTube.

Daniel got home and began spreading the word. Him and Mike created links where people can choose if they want to support the revolution, so that Daniel and Mike can get an idea of how many people would support. After a few days, they had reached over 1 million supporters that would be willing to go to New York City.

The agent began setting up Daniel and Mike on news channels. They appeared on various famous news channels, talk shows, and more, and kept spreading the word. They created tons of advertisements that would be seen worldwide. They hired companies to put up billboards and paper advertisements around major cities. They contacted several airlines that had agreed to offer free flights to New York City. After a month, Mike and Daniel had reached over 1 billion supporters. They were so happy they had so many supporters for such a great cause. They contacted the airplanes and started setting up millions of passengers to depart for New York City. People started planning to fly to New York City to support the revolution. Mike and Daniel had to get the revolution to start soon, because many worldwide were being controlled by Canada and economies were having difficulty supporting the billions of people worldwide as Canada placed many demands on the economy. Many people had been moving out of major cities. Daniel spent many hours praying during these times, and he finally decided he had to do it. He had to start the revolution. To save the world and to find freedom.

CHAPTER 21: FLY

Daniel and Mike got to the nearest airport. They spread the word on their social medias and called the airplane companies to let them know that today was the day they had to invade the Candian Republics headquarters in NYC. The agent let them into the limousine and drove them to the nearest airport. When they got there, it was closed. It had been shut down by the military. "We're gonna have to get a private plane," said Daniel. The agent drove them towards Chase Center and went towards the team plane. Luckily, there was one plane left there. "Well, anyone know how to drive a plane?" asked the agent. "I have some experience," said Daniel. "Great. Good luck, guys. I am proud of you guys for helping the world." said the agent. They thanked each other and got into the private jet. Daniel got into the pilots seat and pulled the lever. The plane started flying forward and up.

Mike calibrated the GPS to go towards New York City. Daniel flew up and found an autopilot button and clicked it. The plane started drifting forwards towards NYC. Daniel went towards the plane's seats and sat next to Mike. He was diligently watching the news.

"We have reports that the revolution of the century is going to begin. It has been reported that the two boys that have started this entire revolution, NBA Superstar Michael Johnson, along with his friend Daniel, are on their way to NYC to talk to Chalito Varat, in order to find freedom for the world. As you can see, many protesters are beginning to arrive at the headquarters in NYC. However, it is being heavily guarded by the Candian militaries, and many airports are being shut down worldwide to stop travel to NYC. We will have more on this soon." said the newsperson.

Mike looked at Daniel. "You ready?" he asked. Daniel nodded. He got up and looked for some food and water in the refrigerator. He drank some water and ate some good meals as he sat in a huge, comfy seat. He looked out of the plane windows and saw clouds and water. He turned on the news.

"As you can see, chaos is beginning to ensue at the NYC headquarters. Many more people are beginning to arrive and protest the unfair controls of Canada. Reports have it that Canadians planes are being sent into the sky to look for Mike and Daniel's plane, the leaders of this movement. Hopefully they are able to stay safe." said the reporter.

Mike and Daniel looked at each other. Just then, Mike's phone started ringing. It was the agent. He answered it and put it on the speakerphone.

"Hey guys, you all safe?" asked the agent.

"Yeah" said Mike and Daniel, cautiously.

"Did you see the news? The Canadians found out you are the leaders of the protest and are now trying to take over your plane. Stay safe." said the agent. He ended the call.

Daniel ran towards the windows. He looked outside and heard the whooshing of what sounded like planes. Just then, he saw multiple planes flying towards his plane. Daniel ran towards the plane controls and turned off the autopilot. He grabbed the steering wheel and steered the plane forward, and faster. Daniel saw the Canadian planes release missiles and collided with the plane. The plane started shaking, and Mike was yelling. Daniel saw the plane was starting to go down. Daniel saw multiple people climbing out of their planes and jumping onto the private plane. He saw the people were holding onto the plane and trying to open the door. Daniel grabbed the steering wheel and steered down. As he got closer, Daniel could see the New York skyline. He saw the headquarters, and thousands, possibly millions, of people crowding around the headquarters and chanting for freedom. Just then, the Canadian planes released another missile as a piece of the private jet broke off. Daniel gripped the steering wheel more as the air from outside rushed in. "Daniel, land quickly!" yelled Mike, holding onto a chair. Daniel steered to the right and saw an airport where he could land nearby. Mike steered towards the airport and saw the Canadian planes following him. He set the private plane in landing mode and landed on the airport runway. After a few seconds, the plane went to a stop. Daniel saw the other planes land nearby. Mike and Daniel jumped out of the plane quickly. They were quickly cornered by multiple soldiers. Daniel looked around quickly. He saw a car. He looked at Mike. They sprinted towards the car. The soldiers started yelling and running after them. Daniel jumped into the driver's seat and Mike got into the passenger's seat. Thankfully, the car key was already in the car. Daniel stepped on the gas and flew forward. Daniel started driving fast towards the NYC headquarters. Mike got the GPS ready to go there. Daniel could see multiple tanks following him. They started shooting missiles. A missile hit the car and the car flew forward. They landed again. Daniel stepped on the gas even more. They drove towards the hills and were driving up the hills towards the city. It was exhilarating. "There!" yelled Mike, pointing towards the HQ. Daniel drove the car in circles to lose the soldiers. Eventually, he parked near some buildings. Mike and Daniel left the car and looked towards the HQ. It was surrounded by millions of protesters. Daniel and Mike ran through the crowd, trying to get into the entrance.

"Everyone, it's Mike and Daniel! Let them through!" yelled some fans.

The protesters stepped aside and gave Mike and Daniel a path towards the HQ. They ran there and were stopped by a group of soldiers. They were surrounded.

Mike and Daniel's attention was drawn to a man, walking slowly towards them, dressed elegantly and followed by multiple bodyguards.

He walked closer to them, and smirked.

It was Chalito Varat. The man who started the Canadian takeover.

"So" he said, with a thick accent. "These are the people.... who are trying to stop me."

His smirk disappeared.

"Pathetic." he said.

"I do respect you for trying to help the world. I really do. But you simply do not understand what I am trying to accomplish. I am trying to help the economies; you just don't understand that, do you?" asked Chalito.

"You're lying!" said Mike boldly, walking forward. Daniel held him back. "You want to take over the economies for your own personal gain! You, filthy, greedy person! Just let the world live in peace! We will give you money, just give us peace!" yelled Mike.

The crowd of protesters were watching in awe.

"You know..." said Varat. "I... I have made over $500 billion dollars so far. People have donated to me, and I promised that I would make the world free If I got what I wanted. Well, I am officially the richest human so far, but that won't stop me. I want more. I won't free the world from Canadian controls." said Chalito.

The crowd gasped. He had been lying.

There was a long silence.

Daniel looked around and saw Mike, staring at Chalito, intensely.

"THEN WE REVOLT! FOR FREEDOM!" yelled Mike.

The crowd started cheering, and everyone started running towards the HQ. It was chaos.

"GET THEM!" yelled Chalito. Mike and Daniel sprinted through the crowd and tried to get inside the HQ. Mike was grabbed by a bodyguard. "Keep going! I'll meet you inside!" yelled Mike. Daniel wanted to help Mike, but he had to help for the world's freedom first. Daniel sprinted inside and got into the HQ. He was surprised by how technologically advanced it was. He sprinted up to the second floor and saw soldiers running after him. Daniel ran towards a sofa and jumped on it and pushed open the vent and crawled inside. He crawled for many minutes, and finally found another opening. He saw another opening and crawled there. It looked like a meeting room, with lots of soldiers in there. They looked like they were forced to work for Chalito, because they were forced. It wasn't fair. As Daniel was looking down through the vents, the vents collapsed. Daniel got up, coughing as dust surrounded the room. The soldiers surrounded him. Daniel got up. He had nowhere to go. He had to talk his way out of this.

"How do you feel, everyone?" said Daniel. "Truly, how do you all feel?" he said. "Do you think this is fair? You are better than this. You know this isn't right. I know it seems like Chalito Varat is controlling you all, but if we revolt, we can have freedom. We can be with our families again. We've made it this far, so let's win this. Let's win this to truly find freedom for the world. Come on, we can do this. We all know that this is the right thing to do. We have the power now. LET US WIN!!" yelled Daniel.

The soldiers started jumping and cheering. They started telling other soldiers the plan. They would pretend to be on Chalito's side but would then make him give freedom to the world.

Daniel gathered the group together and they prayed to God and set out to achieve freedom.

Daniel began walking outside of the room and looking around. He had to find a way to get outside. He ran through the hallways and ran up stairways. Eventually, he got up to the top floor. He went to the patio outside and looked over NYC. Even though it was destroyed, he could see people still had hope. Millions of people were chanting and pushing for freedom. Daniel smiled. He had come such a long way. It was surreal. His story was amazing. "Thank you, God!" said Daniel. Just then, Daniel heard helicopters. He looked back and saw multiple Canadian helicopters land at the top of the HQ. Daniel thought he was going to be taken. And then, he saw Vespucci and multiple other people get out of the helicopters.

"Vespucci!" yelled Daniel, happily. They ran towards each other and hugged. "I saw you on TV at the NBA! I knew you made it!" said Vespucci. Daniel thanked him. "How did you escape from the Canadian controls?" asked Mike. "We convinced the soldiers to push for freedom!" said Vespucci. Now let's revolt for FREEDOM!". The soldiers started cheering. "Ok, everyone try to get inside the building and find Chalito!" yelled Daniel. The soldiers began running through the building looking for Chalito. As Daniel ran in, he heard a robotic voice say, "Lockdown initiated. Mind control activated." from the speaker. Daniel looked around, and saw the windows being closed by metal barriers as the building was literally locking down. He saw soldiers walking stop. They just stopped.

Daniel walked to them, carefully. He could see a device on their heads, beeping. "Mind control activated" said all the soldiers, in unison. Daniel freaked out. He realized the soldiers were literally being mind-controlled. How did Canada have that kind of technology?

All of the soldiers looked at Mike. They started running towards him.

Mike yelled and began running. He ran through various hallways, and could hear the clattering of many feet as people ran after him. Daniel sprinted down staircases. He got to the bottom floor, and saw Mike, hiding behind a sofa. Daniel ran to him and hid behind the sofa too.

"I escaped from the bodyguard" whispered Mike. Daniel said, "I don't know what to do. I am so confused how Chalito has the technology to do this. How could he do this?" said Daniel. "I have no idea" replied Mike. Daniel looked over the sofa and saw multiple soldiers patrolling the area. "We have to get to Chalito. Let's pretend to be soldiers and ask the soldiers where Chalito is." said Daniel. "Great plan." said Johnson. Daniel got up and yelled, "Mind control activated! "All of the soldiers in the room turned and looked at him. After a few seconds, they looked away and kept patrolling the area. Daniel walked up to a soldier. "Excuse me, sir, would you mind telling me where Chalito Varat is?" asked Daniel. The soldier stopped for a second. "Chalito is located on the top floor." Daniel thanked her and ran up to the top floor. Mike carefully followed. Daniel was surprised how easy it was to get past the mind-controlled soldiers. Daniel and Mike got to the top floor and looked around. They saw a huge room and saw 2 people inside. They peeked inside and saw Chalito Varat, talking to Vespucci. "So, you are against my economic ideals, eh?" asked Chalito. Vespucci yelled, "THIS IS NOT RIGHT! FREE THE COUNTRIES FROM YOUR CONTROLS PLEASE!" said Vespucci. Varat laughed. "Well, look at you. Quite passionate for freedom, eh?" said Chalito. "Not for long". Chalito grabbed a mind control device and walked towards Vespucci to put it on him. "No!" yelled Vespucci. Daniel ran into the room. "NO!" yelled Daniel. Chalito stared at him. "YOU!" he said. "Mr. Daniel, huh? You think you are cool, huh?" said Chalito. Daniel noticed Mike sneaking into the room. Luckily, Chalito didn't notice. "I am cool." said Daniel, smirking. "I'm sure you are" responded Chalito. "If I am being honest, I am proud of your confidence. Your confidence to inspire this revolt against my controls. It really takes courage. I am proud of you for that." said Chalito. Daniel looked at Vespucci. "Thank you." said Daniel. He looked over at Vespucci, and he winked at Daniel. He saw Mike crawling around the room, slowly. Daniel had to keep Chalito's attention on him. "So, Chalito, tell me, how are you doing?". Chalito hesitated. "I am fine... and you?" said Chalito. "Doing great!" said Daniel, chuckling. This interaction was very awkward. Daniel just had to keep Chalito distracted, because he knew Mike had a plan. Chalito then got a phone call and walked out of the room for a few seconds. Mike quickly ran to the mind control remote and grabbed it. Chalito ran back into the room. Mike clicked the off button. "Mind control and lockdown deactivated" sounded over the speakers. "NO!" yelled Chalito. He ran towards Mike. Mike dodged him. "Let's go!" he said. Mike ran out of the room, followed by Vespucci and Daniel. They ran downstairs, followed by Chalito Varat. Once they got to the bottom stairs, they ran towards the door. They ran outside and saw the huge crowds of people, still outside and chanting for freedom. They saw multiple soldiers, taking off their mind control devices. "TIME FOR FREEDOM!" yelled Daniel happily. The crowds cheered. Chalito grabbed Daniel firmly and held him in front of the crowds. "Soldiers, take him away." said Chalito. It was quiet for a few seconds. The soldiers didn't move. "Can you hear me? I said take him away!". The soldiers stayed still. "You....are not our leader." said a soldier. She glanced over the crowd. "TIME FOR FREEDOM!" she said. The crowds started cheering and the soldiers ran and grabbed Chalito. They grabbed him and brought him into a military plane. Chalito was yelling at all the soldiers for not obeying him. Daniel was smiling as the plan had worked. Chalito was no longer in control. The goodness of the world wins. Mike and Daniel got into a military plane, and Vespucci was the pilot. He flew over to the United Nations international headquarters nearby in New York City. They landed after a few minutes and got out of the plane. They walked into the headquarters and saw many people, representing many different countries, all in the main meeting room. They all sat down as Chalito Varat was brought into a room. Soldiers held him still as he stood in front of a huge paper.

CHAPTER 22: FREEDOM

"Do you, Chalito Varat, declare to give back the countries of the world their own democratic freedoms, and do you declare to help rebuild and make the world a more equal and better place?" asked the president of the United Nations. There were many cameras and film crews from around the world filming the eventful moment. After minutes of consideration, Chalito Varat said, "Yes.". The people in the room jumped with joy as the world had been given back its freedom. Mike, Daniel, and Vespucci were all cheering. They had helped inspire the revolt for freedom. They were so happy they could help the world out in many ways.

"People around the world are celebrating as Canada no longer has control of the world and its economies! The world is now free! Chalito Varat, Canadians, and people all around the world are uniting to help rebuild the world and to work for a better world. A major part of the revolution was from Mike and Daniel, who helped inspire the NYC revolutions. Congratulations to them for their massive successes! Thank you all for watching, keep working on your goals, love one another, be grateful and humble, and most importantly, God Bless!" said the newsperson very happily.

Daniel smiled. After the revolution was won, he went home to a huge parade celebrating his successes. He thanked all the people for all their support. He thanked Mike for helping him get famous and helping him find a house. He thanked Vespucci for raising him and inspiring him to improve his life and others and to succeed in life and to help others do the same as well.

And most importantly, he thanked Jesus. For always Being There for him. For always Supporting him. For always Believing in him. For always Loving him. For giving him Purpose.

Daniel was amazed at how his life was going, in a good way. He had been through so much, and he had more to go through, bad and good. He knows life is a journey, and that there will be bad days and good days. However, he knows how to stay positive and to keep working to become the best version of himself, and to help other people become the best versions of themselves. Daniel was so thankful for how his journey was going, and he couldn't wait to see what the future was going to be like for him. Daniel smiled as he sat in his house, overlooking all of Los Angeles. He could see the happiness in the people's faces. He could see the love between the many communities. He knew he didn't have his life solved, but he knew he would continue to work for his passions. He had made it so far in life and would keep striving for the best of the best the world has to offer. Daniel picked up his Holy Bible and continued reading. Jesus is King.

A Message For You

Thank you so much for reading this book! I really hope you enjoyed it and thank you for supporting charities. You are amazing for that! Now, I don't know what you are going through. It may seem difficult, but it isn't meant to be easy, but it will be worth it. One day, it will all make sense, and you will truly be happy and fulfill your potential. However, the choice is up to you. I know this has been said a lot, but never give up. Never give up. We all have dreams, but not many achieve their dreams, because they are quite simply difficult to achieve. When you feel like your dreams are too difficult, think about how happy you will be once you achieve them. You have to put in effort into all your goals to achieve them. You shouldn't compare yourself to others, you can be motivated by them, but go for self improvements to truly definitely improve. You can do this! You were created by God for a Reason. You have Purpose. Always be kind, always be humble, and be the best version of yourself. Stay positive and as you walk through bad days and good days, keep working for your goals. If you keep working, you will achieve your goals. God sent his only son, Jesus Christ, to die and rise for us. Clearly, God and Jesus love us so much. Make Them proud by achieving your dreams. Always be a good person and bring out the best in other people too. I really wish the best for you. And remember, God is always on your side. Jesus loves you!!

"Believe you can and you're halfway there."

– Theodore Roosevelt

"Wake up determined, go to bed satisfied."

— Dwayne "The Rock" Johnson

"Life is like riding a bicycle. To keep your balance, you must keep moving."

– Albert Einstein

"Be the best version of yourself in anything that you do. You don't have to live anybody else's story."

-Stephen Curry

"Success is not in what you have, but in who you are."

-

Jeremiah 29:11

"For I know the plans I have for you." declares the Lord, "plans to prosper you and not to harm you, plans to give you hope and a future.

Joshua 1:9

Have I not commanded you? Be strong and courageous. Do not be afraid; do not be discouraged, for the LORD your God will be with you wherever you go."

Phillipians 4:13

"I can do all things through Christ who strengthens me."

Mark 10:27

Jesus looked at them and said, "With man this is impossible, but not with God; all things are possible with God."

John 16:33

"I have told you these things, so that in me you may have peace. In this world you will have trouble. But take heart! I have overcome the world."